"What's going on with you and Jon Madison?" Cindy asked eagerly when she saw me outside of class.

"Nothing important." We began walking toward our lockers. "He and my brother are going to play a correspondence game of chess." I explained the way it worked to her, and she looked impressed.

"Two megabrains, that's what they are," she said. Then she turned and stared at me. "How do you fit into all this? Have you suddenly decided that Jon is cuter than Luke?"

I gave her a withering look. "You've got to be kidding. Luke Russell is one of the best-looking guys in the whole school."

"Yeah, but he's not exactly one of the smartest," Cindy replied.

"So? Maybe that's the type I go for." I raised my chin a little bit, to show I was serious. "I don't belong with the intellectuals, and I'm smart enough to know it."

It was odd. I'd said that line many times before, but just then I was having trouble convincing myself it was true.

Bantam Sweet Dreams Romances
Ask your bookseller for the books you have missed

Playing Games

Eileen Hehl

BANTAM BOOKS
TORONTO · NEW YORK · LONDON · SYDNEY · AUCKLAND

RL 6, IL age 11 and up

PLAYING GAMES
A Bantam Book / July 1986

ISBN 0-553-25642-4

Published simultaneously in the United States and Canada

Bantam Books are published by Bantam Books, Inc. Its trademark, consisting of the words "Bantam Books" and the portrayal of a rooster, is registered in U.S. Patent and Trademark Office and in other countries. Marca Registrada. Bantam Books, Inc., 666 Fifth Avenue, New York, New York 10103.

Printed and bound in Great Britain by Hunt Barnard Printing Ltd.

O   0 9 8 7 6 5 4 3 2 1

Playing Games

Chapter One

Puppies! It seemed I was buried in them as I drove along Main Street that Tuesday morning in my mother's little Mazda.

There I was, trying to drive with some dignity, and those two wiggling, yelping puppies were making it impossible. I had Pillbox, my terrier mutt, caught up in my hair, and Marietta, my neighbor's sheepdog puppy, trying to stand on my lap and stick her nose out the window.

I wasn't managing to control them too well.

"Kerry, I'm afraid you won't be able to handle both of those puppies and drive, too," my mom had said when I started out, but I

1

was sure that I could. What a mistake that had been!

Both puppies had been tied on leashes in the backseat. But somehow the leashes had come undone, and just then I was being strangled as I tried to drive. I must have looked like an escapee from the funny farm.

Give it up, Kerry, I told myself, and pulled the car over. It was typical of me to get into an airhead situation like that.

Just then I saw Jon Madison, a boy from school, standing alone at his bus stop. I had seen the school bus go by at least ten minutes earlier. *Poor guy,* I thought. Jon was one of those super genius types, but sometimes those brainy people aren't very practical.

"Hey!" I called out. "I hate to tell you this, but I think you missed the bus. Want a ride to school?"

Jon came over to the car and peered in. He looked shocked when he saw me, a crazy girl with wild, red-blond hair, trying to subdue two impossible, hyperactive pups.

"I know this looks a little strange," I began. Just then Marietta jumped back on my chest with a thump. "Ooof. Yuck. I really *am* going to Lincoln High School—I just have to take— aaargh—" At that moment Pillbox leaped over my shoulder and into the backseat, nearly taking my left ear with her.

"Did you say the school bus has already gone by?" Jon Madison certainly wasn't hard of hearing, but maybe being in such a state of shock had made him a little slow at catching on. "And did you say you're offering me a ride to—er—school?"

"Sure." I beamed at him to show that I wasn't really crazy. "I'm Kerry Fields. I'm in your English class."

"Oh. You look as though you could use some help." Jon opened the car door and got in. He held Marietta firmly, which was not an easy thing to do. But she evidently liked being disciplined. She began to lick him with great enthusiasm.

Not to be outdone, Pillbox scrambled toward the interesting new passenger. So now it was Jon who was buried in puppies, and I knew I had to do something about it—fast.

"I'm sorry about all this." I reached for Pillbox's leash. "They're supposed to be tied to the seat belts in back."

"*Why?*" Jon asked, looking from me to the puppies and back again. He was trying to hold Marietta at bay with both arms.

"You mean why do I have them in the car?" I

3

was leaning over in the back, snapping the belt buckle tightly on Pillbox.

"Yes." He fended off another slurp from Marietta. "Why are you transporting these wild canines?"

"They're going to the vet's—to be spayed."

"Both of them? Are they both yours?"

I laughed. "No, no, no. That one," I said, pointing to Marietta, "belongs to my neighbor. Mrs. Perlowsky asked me if I'd mind taking her puppy to the clinic as long as Pillbox was going."

"Pillbox? You actually have a dog named Pillbox?" Jon chuckled. It was the first time I'd heard Jon laugh. He had a really nice laugh, rich and deep, and I remember thinking, *Maybe he's not such a nerd, after all.*

I laughed, too. With the puppies secured, I went back to driving, but once in a while I stole a look over at Jon on the pretext of watching Marietta.

He's not bad-looking at all, I thought. *Why did I ever think he was a nerd? Because he's smart and wears glasses?*

Actually Jon was cute in a lot of ways. He was tall, with a nice lean, honest-looking face. His dark hair was overly curly and probably could've used a good cut, but I thought it made him seem like a prominent classical conductor.

Yes, he's definitely cute, I decided. But I also knew he was definitely not my type.

Jon's IQ had to be at least as high as my brother Bill's. And I was one girl who never intended to get involved with a genius.

"Here we are," I said, noticing the relief on Jon's face. The Briarwood Animal Hospital was right on the way to school. I stopped the car and hurried out, dragging Pillbox with me, while Jon somehow managed to get Marietta's leash under control. He followed along behind me.

"Good morning, Kerry," called out Dr. Turner, the elderly, white-haired veterinarian. "What have we got here? Are these the two customers you told me about?"

"Yes. This one here is Pillbox, and the other one is Marietta," I said, and rushed Pillbox to a cage in the back room. Again, Jon followed me.

"How do you know your way around here so well?" Jon asked. "Do you work here or something?"

"I have for two summers." I was proud of it, too. My job at the animal hospital was the first one I'd ever had; I'd gotten it just after I turned sixteen. I didn't tell Jon that my main function had been to walk the dogs and clean the cages. He'd think I was a dummy if I did.

"I'm impressed," he said with admiration. "This is a nice place to work. It's much more lively than my summer job."

What job? I wondered, but Marietta distracted me before I could ask. I took her from Jon and plunked her into a cage of her own.

"Well, so long for now, girls," I called out to the puppies. "Don't think it's been fun—because it hasn't."

Jon's eyes met mine, and he must have also been thinking about the crazy car ride we had just endured with those puppies. We both started laughing.

"Sounds like a circus back here," Dr. Turner declared, entering the kennel room. But I knew he didn't mind. He was a nice, relaxed man, and I knew that he trusted my judgment. Most of the time, anyway.

"There. I told you I'd get you to school on time," I said proudly as we edged into a tiny parking space behind Lincoln High. Jon looked a little green.

"Er . . . thanks, er, Kerry." Shaking his head, he jumped out of the car. I didn't think I'd been driving that fast, but Jon acted sort of the way someone does after a wild rollercoaster ride. He seemed afraid that the car might start up again and take him for another trip.

But I'm not a bad driver. I may not be brainy like Jon or my brother, Bill, but I know the things I can do well. And driving is one of them.

Anyway, that was all I saw of Jon Madison that day, until English class. He smiled vaguely, as though he'd never seen me before in his life.

"So there I was with puppies jumping all over me when I noticed this guy, Jon Madison, standing at his bus stop—" I was telling my brother about my morning as we both slaved away at mowing and raking our front yard. Thankfully it was September, and we wouldn't have to cut the lawn much longer.

"Jon Madison?" Bill asked with interest. "I didn't know you knew him."

"I do now, I guess." *And he thinks I'm a complete dingbat*, I added silently.

"I've heard a lot about him. He's supposed to be a real whiz at chess, among other things."

"Really? Imagine that." One thing I wasn't up on was the latest school genius. I had enough trouble keeping up with my own crowd—the semismart and the semiathletic.

"Yes, Jon Madison. I'm sure that's the guy I heard about." Bill scooped up a pile of grass clippings and stuffed them into a large plastic bag; Mom had asked us to save the clippings for her garden mulch. "So you do know him?"

"I guess I do now." I finished telling him the story of the puppies.

Bill grinned, which made him look younger than he really was. Bill was a junior at the nearby Polytechnic Institute, pulling all A's of course, and heading for a great future as an electrical engineer. He also rated all A's as a brother.

"You probably think the kid is a nerd, don't you, Kerry?" Bill scolded. He was always trying to teach me not to put labels on people. "I was just thinking—I'd like to challenge him to a chess game."

"So go ahead," I said, shrugging. I was wishing that we didn't have to do all that yard work. I'd much rather have been out taking pictures. That semester, I was taking an advanced photography course, and I was really getting enthusiastic about it. I'd used all my earnings from my job at the animal hospital to buy a secondhand 35-mm camera and darkroom equipment.

Bill was still talking about chess. "Kerry, I don't mean a face-to-face game. I don't have enough time for that right now. What I'm talking about is a correspondence game—have you heard of that?"

"No," I said as I started fighting with the lawn mower. It was the kind of mower that would start easily for men and boys, but never for girls. And I was determined to change that curse.

"You don't know how to start that mower," Bill began, but I gave him an angry glare that made him step back a few paces.

"I'm *going* to start it," I declared. I grabbed the start cord and pulled. And pulled. I tried to snap it, the way I'd seen Dad and Bill do. It's all in the wrist, they always told me. But my wrist action, I was finding out, just didn't cut it.

"Lousy male chauvinist lawn mower," I grumbled, aware that I was beginning to sweat from the effort.

"I can do it for you—"

"*No!*" I spat back. At that outburst, Bill jumped out of my way, looking highly amused. I must admit I'd sounded like a madwoman.

"Well, while you're trying to master that machine, can I tell you about the correspondence game? Kerry? Are you listening?"

"Sure," I grunted, yanking on the cord again.

"If he accepts my challenge, you'd be the

9

go-between—if you don't object, that is. You would take my chess move to Jon, and when he decides on *his* move, you'd bring it home to me."

I kicked the lawn mower, hard, but it only made my foot hurt. "Sounds as though I'd be the pawn in the middle," I commented, feeling increasingly angry. "Suppose I don't feel like talking to this guy every day in school?"

"Ah, Kerry, you'd do it for me, wouldn't you? Your favorite brother?"

"You're my *only* brother, and I don't know, Bill. I do have my own life to live." I knew I'd do it, but I hoped he'd try to bribe me if I held out.

He didn't disappoint me. "I'd probably let you use my car more often, sister dear—"

"Well, that sounds like a good deal." I smiled broadly. "And on top of that—will you please start this stubborn old mower before I go crazy?"

"No problem," Bill said in a deliberate, completely obnoxious tone of voice. "No problem at all, little lady." And just like that, he reached out and started the mower.

Chapter Two

Because I was late to English class the next day, I didn't have a chance to talk to Jon about Bill's chess game. I sprinted through the door just after the bell rang, and slid into my seat.

"Late again, Miss Fields," whispered my best friend Cindy Kraft.

"Late again, Miss Fields," echoed Mr. Bandero, the English teacher. Fortunately, Mr. Bandero was a pretty cool guy, and I didn't think he would put me down for detention.

"I have a reason—" I began.

"You *always* have a reason," the teacher said and sighed. "And your excuses are highly creative, Miss Fields. But I think we'll skip

11

hearing about it this time. You can use your imagination in a more constructive way."

He then asked us each to write a short essay, in class. The topic was "What I Want to Do with My Life." We'd been writing about that same theme every year since we were freshmen, but each English teacher always wanted us to write about it again. They said it would help us see how our writing skills had improved.

I wrote my essay about my ambition to be a photographer. Two years before, I'd written about my future as a marine biologist, and the year before that I had wanted to be a veterinarian.

Well, we all have different dreams at different times.

But I was serious about my most recent career choice. I planned to study photography in college and someday be a free-lance photographer, selling my work to magazines and newspapers.

And eventually there would be books, too. They would be the kind you see on the coffee tables of rich, discriminating people: *China*, photographed by Kerry Fields; *Inside the Kremlin*, by Kerry Fields; *An American's Viewpoint of Paris*, by— and so on.

We passed in our papers, and Mr. Bandero

said there was time to read a few of them out loud. The second one he read was mine.

"All right," he said, after he'd read it. "What could be done to improve this essay?"

Nobody's hand went up. It was the end of the day, and everyone was tired and looking forward to getting out of school. Besides, everybody knew that it was my essay, even though my name hadn't been mentioned. I was famous at Lincoln High School for my exploits with the camera. My friends even called me Kerry the Flash.

"I'd like comments from someone, please." Mr. Bandero was trying to be very stern and serious, even though he probably wanted to leave as much as we did.

Jon Madison raised his hand. Either he didn't know that the essay was mine, or he recognized Kerry the Flash and just didn't care.

"Yes, Jon?" the teacher said eagerly.

Jon stood up. "That was a good essay."

I beamed. Cindy turned and smiled at me.

"But the writer's scope was rather limited, I believe," Jon continued.

"Would you care to expand on that?"

"All the writer talked about was the career he or she planned. He or she made no mention of other things in life—family, surroundings, hobbies."

"A valid point. Anyone care to comment on that?"

My face burning, I raised my hand. "Maybe the writer of that essay was only thinking of one thing at a time," I said defensively. "Maybe whoever wrote it is not a computer brain who can juggle millions of ideas at once."

Jon looked at me with surprise. It must have dawned on him right then that it was *my* essay we were discussing.

"Perhaps you're right," he said in a quiet voice, then sat down.

Instantly I was sorry for what I'd said. I did have a right to defend my essay, but maybe I'd been a little too insulting. I hadn't meant to say all that; it had just come out. And then, too late, I'd remembered that my brother wanted me to befriend this guy!

I went over to him as soon as English class was over. "Jon—" I began.

"Don't apologize. I deserved it." He blinked his eyes. They were a very light gray, and somehow they made him look vulnerable. It was as though you could see right into his thoughts. I've always been fascinated by light eyes like that.

"Oh, I wasn't going to apologize," I blurted

out. *Whoops,* I thought, *I've said the wrong thing again, haven't I?* I tried to start again. "You *are* a computer brain, Jon, and you should be proud of it. Besides, I wanted to ask you something else. This is a proposition—or a challenge—from my brother."

I explained about Bill being a junior at Polytech as well as a pretty hot chess player. Then I mentioned that Bill wanted to start a correspondence chess game with him. I asked Jon if he'd ever heard of correspondence games before; *I* certainly never had, until now.

"Of course. It's done all the time." Jon smiled. How different he looked when he smiled! I thought. It reminded me of the day before at the animal hospital when we'd been laughing. The nerd look was completely gone. Jon was actually good-looking, just as I'd suspected when I'd looked at him in the car.

"I'd love to accept your brother's challenge," he said simply.

"Great. I'll be the go-between. I guess I'm even the pawn, if you can stand the pun."

"Yes, the humble pawn. Never underestimate the lowly pawn," Jon said with great seriousness. He looked at me with interest. "Why are you doing this?"

"Why? For my brother, who's a good guy. And because he'll lend me his car if I do." I grinned. "It's nice to have wheels when you're a busy photographer."

John just smiled back and nodded. Again I felt stupid, as if my getting to use Bill's car was silly and frivolous. Maybe superbrains like Jon just couldn't understand someone like me, someone who had no more ambition in life than to take pictures. I suppose it must have seemed a puny goal, when he was probably on his way to being the top research scientist in the world.

He scooped up his books, and we walked toward the door. "How are those puppies?" he asked with genuine concern. "Did their operations go all right?"

"Sure. Absolutely. Dr. Turner is a really terrific vet. I think Pillbox is kind of sad, though. Now she'll never be a mother."

Jon laughed.

"Oh, Bill says it's your move first," I remembered. "It's something about your being white."

Jon looked amused. "You're not a chess player, are you, Kerry."

Well, I thought with surprise, *at least he remembered my name.*

"Me? No. But don't worry, I'll deliver your moves accurately. And, listen—you can probably expect my brother to beat you. He's usually

16

invincible." I was glad I'd thought of that word. It sounded rather intellectual.

"Is he?" Again, Jon got that amused look on his face. "We'll see about that."

"What's with you and Jon Madison?" Cindy asked eagerly when she saw me. She had been waiting outside the door of the English classroom. "Come on, Kerry, what gives?"

"Nothing important." We began walking toward our lockers. "He and my brother are going to play a correspondence game of chess, that's all." I explained the whole thing to Cindy, and she looked impressed.

"Two megabrains, that's what they are. I wonder which one will win?" she said absently. Then she turned and stared at me. "And what's your interest in all this, anyway? Have you suddenly decided Jon is cuter than Luke?"

I gave her a withering look. "You've got to be kidding. Luke Russell is one of the best-looking guys in the whole school."

"Yeah, but he's also one of the dumbest, and you know it."

"So? Maybe that's the type I go for." I raised my chin a little bit, to show that I was serious. "You know I would never want to go out with anyone who's really smart."

17

Cindy was pretty smart herself, a model student. "Well, I guess I can see your point, Kerry. But I think you've just lived in the shadow of your brother too long."

"No, it's that I don't belong with the intellectuals, and I'm smart enough to know it." It was odd. I had said that line many times before, but just then I was having trouble convincing myself it was true.

"Hi, Kerry," Luke Russell called out as we approached him. He was waiting at my locker for me, as he often did. He nodded hello to Cindy. "You look pretty today, Kerry."

I do? I thought with astonishment. I was wearing an outfit that my mother called my gypsy costume—a calf-length denim skirt with a brightly patterned scarf at the waist, and a white peasant blouse with billowing sleeves. Every now and then I liked to wear something really crazy, but I had my more conservative moments, too. Looking exactly the same every day seemed so boring.

I guess trying to be different was the story of my life. My strawberry-blond hair is so unruly that I could never look ordinary, anyway. So I decided early on that I'd cultivate a style all my own. And my unusual hair helps. Sometimes I let it bush out naturally. Otherwise, I braid it or tie it back in a ponytail.

18

"You're never conventional, Kerry," Cindy once told me. "I guess that's the artistic photographer in you."

I'd shrugged and said, "I was born too late to be a beatnik or a hippie. And I don't think I'm the punk type. So the best I can strive for is different."

My thoughts were interrupted when I noticed that Luke was looking at me as though I were a gorgeous model or something. A girl can't help being flattered by such obvious devotion.

I turned to open my locker, and Luke sort of shuffled his feet. "So—have you asked anybody to the Sadie Hawkins Dance yet, Kerry?"

I looked at him in surprise. I hadn't even thought about the dance. It was an annual event, held sometime in October or November, to which girls got to ask the boys, just like in the old comic strip with Li'l Abner.

"No," I said slowly, taking a long time to choose the books I'd need from my locker.

"Well, if you asked me, we could double-date with Cindy and Phil."

"Cindy and Phil?" I asked, turning to stare at Cindy. "You invited Phil to the Sadie Hawkins?"

Cindy blushed. "I guess I forgot to mention it to you."

Phil was a good friend of Luke's, and Cindy had had a crush on him for ages. I couldn't believe she had invited him without telling me.

"I'll bet you forgot." I stared at the two of them. "This sounds more like a conspiracy to me."

Cindy and Luke laughed. "So we wanted to get something up for the dance," Luke admitted. "That's not so terrible is it?"

"No." *No,* I thought, *it isn't so bad, except that it's the Sadie Hawkins Dance, and the girl is supposed to choose her date.* Instead, I was being railroaded into a date that I hadn't picked.

"Oh, well. Everyone knows you can't fight city hall," I said, and smiled in spite of myself. "Luke, how *would* you like to be my date for the Sadie Hawkins Dance?"

His handsome face lit up with happiness. "I thought you'd never ask!"

I slammed my locker door, feeling let down all of a sudden. And I couldn't figure out why. There was no one else I would have invited. Luke was the only boy I'd been dating recently.

Just then, Jon Madison appeared, to hand me a slip of paper.

"White's first move," he said, then quickly disappeared into the traffic of kids in the hall.

"White's first move?" Luke looked confused. "What's he talking about?"

The three of us looked at the slip of paper. *P—E4* was scribbled across it.

"Jon and I have a secret mission," I whispered conspiratorially. "We're plotting to overthrow the board of education."

Cindy and I burst into giggles, and Luke just shook his head.

Chapter Three

"What in the world does it mean?" I asked Bill that evening as I handed him the scrap of paper Jon had given me. "It looks like some kind of code," I said.

Bill smiled. "It means just what it says. Pawn to E4."

"*Bill,*" I cried, giving him one of my I-will-murder-you looks. "Can't you explain it in terms that normal human beings can understand?"

"Sure, Kerry. Well, for starters." He motioned to the chessboard that he kept set up on a small table in the corner of our living room. We walked over to it. "The chessboard is divided up into all these squares."

"Oh, wow. Even I know that much."

He gave me his Bill-will-explain look. "And each one of the squares is assigned a number and a letter for exact identification. Understand? These squares are labeled A, B, C, D, up to H." He swept his hand across the top of the board. "And we go down this side for the numbers, one through eight."

"Oh. That I didn't know."

"It's a coordinate system for recording games. Each piece has a symbol. Like P for pawn, and K for king."

"Q for queen?" I asked.

"Yes," Bill said. "N for knight, R for rook, and so on."

"Wow. It's pretty simple. I can't believe I couldn't figure it out."

"You were never interested before," Bill countered. "And that doesn't mean you're dumb. There are a lot of things you know that I don't know. Or Jon Madison, either, for that matter."

"Oh, *sure.*" I made a sarcastic face. But then I was curious. "Like what?"

Bill leaned back lazily against the bookcase wall. "Oh, lots of things. Like what Bruce Springsteen was wearing when you saw him in concert, or where Rob Lowe goes for vacation, or what color Cyndi Lauper's hair is these days."

I tried to swat him, but he moved too quickly. "Gee, thanks," I said. "You make me sound like a flea-brain."

"You're not. You read those picture magazines from cover to cover because you're interested in celebrities. There's nothing wrong with that. You'll be a famous photograher someday because you care about what other people think and like and want to know about."

"Big deal," I grumbled, wondering why I felt so depressed.

Bill stared at me oddly but didn't say anything.

I looked away from him and down at the chessboard. I took a white pawn and moved it to where I thought E4 should be. "Is that the right place, Bill? I mean, the place where Jon is moving his pawn?"

"Yep."

So, I had learned a little bit about chess. Maybe I wasn't such a dummy, after all.

"I hope you beat Jon," I said unexpectedly. "He's awfully sure of himself, you know."

Bill was studying my face. "Maybe he has reason to be."

*　　*　　*

I was scrunched underneath Mr. Bandero's desk in English class the next time I saw Jon Madison.

"Uh—Kerry, is that you?"

I spotted the shoes first and leaned forward, looking up until I saw Jon's face. He had a perplexed expression.

I laughed. "I suppose I must look a little strange."

"No," he replied, smiling. "Not at all. Not for you, anyway."

I tried to tell if he was being sarcastic, but I don't think he was. He looked as though he was enjoying talking to a goofy girl hiding underneath a desk.

"Well, I do have a reason for being here," I explained.

"And your reasons are usually highly creative," Jon said, sounding like Mr. Bandero. He crouched down and gave me a lopsided grin. "So—do you have any puppies under there with you?" His beautiful gray eyes twinkled at me from behind his glasses.

"Of course not."

"I didn't really think you did. But seriously, Kerry, I wondered if you had your brother's chess move yet?"

"Oh, yes I do. But it's in my locker, so I'll

have to give it to you later." I was getting my camera ready as I spoke.

Jon watched me quietly for a minute. "OK, I give up. I have to ask. *Why* are you underneath this desk?" There was a chuckle in his voice.

With great dignity, I said, "I plan to get a surprise photograph of Mr. Bandero. For the yearbook."

"Oh." Jon blinked. "Of course. I should have guessed."

"Don't act as if you're humoring me," I said impatiently. "This is a good way to get him, when he's not expecting me. Sometimes I like to get a picture that's not posed."

"You're quite a character, Kerry," Jon said in a cheerful way. "Is your brother anything like you?"

"No," I said. "Absolutely not. Bill is really smart and serious, I told you that. A real intellectual."

"But I meant—is he kind of nutty, sometimes?"

"Bill?" I thought about it for a moment. "Yes, I suppose so. I mean, he has a good sense of humor. But"—I grinned—"I don't think you would ever find him underneath a teacher's desk."

"Or driving around in a car full of puppies?"

"Come on, it was just two little puppies. Hey, you'd better get out of the way. I think I hear Mr. Bandero's voice down the hall."

Jon stood up. I heard him muttering something like, "I wouldn't want to get in the way of an artist at work," as he went to his seat.

Mr. Bandero came into the room along with a bunch of kids. He was talking to a couple of them about the homework assignment. I waited until just the right moment and then popped up from my hiding spot.

My flashbulb went off, and the whole class began clapping, shouting, and whistling.

"Kerry the Flash strikes again," someone said, and we were all laughing as I took my seat. Mr. Bandero shook his head as though he'd never known such a weird girl in his whole life. But I could tell he didn't mind. He was flattered, I think, that someone would go to so much trouble to get his picture.

I stole a quick look at Jon. He was sitting quietly at his desk, watching. He had an odd look on his face, and I couldn't quite place it. But it seemed kind of *approving*.

But that's crazy, I told myself. *How can Jon approve of me?* He'd said I was nutty. He always seemed to find me doing something off-the-wall.

Still, I felt warm inside thinking he might

think I'd done something well. After all, if a genius like Jon approved of me—if he *did*, that is—then I couldn't be too hopelessly dumb, could I?

After the class had settled down, I scribbled a note to Jon. "Where will you be after school? I'll bring Bill's chess move there."

He looked surprised when the note landed on his desk. He seemed to get a kick out of receiving in-class mail. He wrote back, "I'll be in the computer room."

Naturally, I thought. It was just the sort of place where Bill could usually be found, too. They certainly were alike.

Well, Kerry, I thought, *you may as well forget about Jon and his fascinating gray eyes. He's too smart for you, and you know it. You'll only get in trouble if you let yourself start liking a superbrain like your brother.*

I was very cool and detached when I took Bill's chess move up to the computer room. Sedate, and absolutely normal—almost.

"Here you are, Jon," I said, interrupting him as he programmed some sort of complicated formula into one of the school computers.

"Oh. Thanks, Kerry." He looked down at the chess move on the paper. "Aha! Your brother is a shrewd one," he observed.

"Bill knows what he's doing." I spoke crisply.

"Uh, Kerry. I hate to say this, but—do you realize your shirt is buttoned crooked?"

I stared down at my shirt. "Of course I realize it. It's supposed to be that way. Don't you ever pay attention to fashion?" I knew he could tell I was lying, but he didn't say so.

"Oh. I guess you know more about those things than I do." Jon looked back down at the keyboard.

"Yes, I do." All my coolness and calmness was leaving me. Why did he have to notice my shirt? I must have buttoned it wrong after gym class. No matter what I did, I was doomed to be a flake forever.

"I have to go," I said quickly. "To the darkroom, to develop some pictures. "Bye, now."

I fled from the computer room. Behind me I could swear I heard that soft chuckle of Jon's echoing in the big, empty room.

I really did go to the photography room, stopping in the girls' room first to fix my shirt. Most of Mr. Shannon's advanced photography students used the darkroom at school, so it was a popular hangout for camera buffs.

"Kerry, I'm glad you came by," Mr. Shannon said when I popped my head in the door.

"Why, what's up?"

Everyone liked Mr. Shannon. He was small, a little overweight, and genial, except when he taught his regular subject, which was calculus—a subject I never intended to study.

"Kerry, you're doing some fine work this year." He pointed to a folder that held some of my most recent photos. "You really are doing yourself proud with these puppy pictures."

I blushed with pleasure. "Thanks, Mr. Shannon. How did you know I needed a few kind words today?"

"I know you're quite serious about your photos, Kerry, so I just wanted to tell you you're on the right track. And I wanted to be sure you're planning to submit something to this contest."

He handed me an application form.

"Oh, that statewide contest?" I read the paper out loud. " 'We are accepting photographs on any topic, taken by students of photography who are in good standing in their courses at any high school in the state. . . .' " I looked up at him. "Sounds good. But there will be a lot of competition, I'll bet."

"Of course there will." Mr. Shannon grinned kindly. "But they'll have to be pretty good to beat our Kerry the Flash. I heard about your latest feat in Mr. Bandero's class," he added.

"Popping out from under the desk. Good for you! You certainly have a way of accomplishing your goals, Kerry."

I felt really great when he said that. It wasn't often that I felt I deserved praise. I guess it came from being Bill Fields's little sister, and always being sort of second-best. Whatever the reason, Mr. Shannon's words gave me hope that maybe I'd turn out to be somebody, someday, after all.

"I'll work on getting something to submit to this contest, Mr. Shannon," I promised, giving him a smile.

And I would, too. I'd find a way to prove to myself—and the whole school—that Kerry Fields was more than just a flaky kid with a camera.

Chapter Four

I cleaned up my act for a few days after that. No more running around with my shirt on wrong and no more hiding under desks.

I also had a lot of homework in history and biology, so even though I had my camera with me all the time, I tried to concentrate on schoolwork, for a change.

It was dull. Even Mr. Bandero said one day, "What's this, Kerry? You handed in your homework assignment on time, and you're not in the middle of some crazy scheme to take someone's picture. What's going on?"

"She's probably running a fever, Mr. B.,"

Cindy told him with a straight face. "Maybe we'd better rush her off to the nurse's office."

Every kid in the room laughed.

"You weren't even late to class today—or yesterday." Mr. Bandero stared at me from under his thick, bushy eyebrows. "This sounds mighty serious to me."

I shrugged, trying not to let my face get too red. "Sometimes people just change, Mr. B.," I said philosophically. At that my classmates really roared, making enough noise to be heard outside in the halls. And when I looked over at Jon, he was laughing with the rest of them.

Why should it matter to me what he thinks, anyway? I asked myself.

I saw Jon each day in English, of course, but I only spoke to him for the minute it took to hand the chess moves back and forth.

Jon and Bill were really into the game. Every other day, no matter how busy Bill was, he studied the chessboard and scribbled down a move for me to give Jon. And the same went for Jon. When it was his turn, he never failed to come back with some kind of strategic attack. The game was solemn business with those two.

The funny part was, Luke Russell still didn't know what was going on. He'd see me conferring with Jon, and he'd come charging after me to ask me why "that nerd" kept talking to me.

One Friday afternoon, when Jon came over to me in the cafeteria, he sat down beside me instead of just handing over his move for Bill. Luke, who was sitting two tables away with his friends, glared over at us.

"How're you doing, Kerry?" Jon asked, just as naturally as though we'd been good friends for years. I didn't want to feel my heart go thunking around in my chest when I looked at him, so I tried to concentrate on the salad I was having for lunch.

"Fine. And you?" Oops, I looked up by mistake and caught a glimpse of his face. It was such an absolutely handsome face, I thought. He should have been all pasty-white or undernourished or something, from devoting all his time to studies. Instead, here was this healthy, cheerful boy with no flaws—unless you considered glasses a flaw. I didn't.

"Oh, I'm fine," he answered. He sat back in his chair, comfortable and unaware that he was getting the evil eye from Luke. "I just wanted to ask you to please tell your brother that I'm really enjoying this chess game. I hadn't known what to expect, but it's definitely a challenge."

"I'll tell him," I said, pleased.

"I hope to meet him someday," Jon went on. "If he ever has the time for a real game, that would be great."

"Sure. Well, Bill is really busy. Polytech is a hard school, you know."

"I know. That's where I want to go." Jon was a senior like me, and I wasn't surprised to learn that he had his college—and probably his whole future—all planned out. Polytech was one of the best schools in the country.

I felt so dumb, thinking about the colleges that I planned to apply to, schools that offered a lot of art and photography courses.

"Maybe Bill could show you around the Polytech campus sometime," I said. "It's old, and it's sort of ugly, but in a way it's very impressive. So serious, you know."

"Sure. I've seen some of it, but I'd love to have a real tour, especially from a student." Jon was interrupted just then by Luke, who had come over to our table.

"OK, just what's going on here?" Luke was trying to keep his voice light and joking, but he didn't quite succeed.

I laughed. "I told you before, Luke. Jon and I are planning a big takeover. We've decided to kidnap the superintendent of schools and hold all the custodians for hostages."

36

Luke kept staring at us. "Come on, Kerry, knock it off."

"Oh, Luke, I was only kidding. Why are you so angry with me?" I asked.

"I'll tell you why. Because you and this nerd are getting too close lately." Then he turned to Jon. "What is it you want with Kerry, anyway?" Luke demanded. "You trying to get her to ask you to the Sadie Hawkins Dance tomorrow night? Because if that's it, you're too late." He beamed and put an arm around my shoulders. "She already asked me."

"Is that so?" Jon looked at me with surprise. "Well, well."

"Luke Russell, you're making a fool of yourself," I snapped. "The truth is—not that it's any of your business, really, but I'll tell you— Jon is playing a correspondence chess game with my brother Bill."

"Besides," Jon added in a mild voice, "I've already been invited to the Sadie Hawkins Dance." He pushed his chair back and stood up.

You have? I wanted to ask.

Suddenly I was dying of curiosity. Who had asked him to the dance? Somehow I had never thought of Jon as a boy who'd go to high-school dances. He had always seemed so far above that kind of thing. But obviously some-one had seen him in a different light.

Who is it? I wondered. I gritted my teeth and realized that I probably wouldn't know until the dance the next night.

After Jon walked away, I turned angrily to Luke. "Listen to me, Luke. Don't you ever be rude like that to any of my friends again. You don't own me, and I can talk to anyone I want without having to explain it to you."

"You're right, Kerry. I'm sorry. It's just that I like you so much."

He looked truly sorry. Poor Luke. He was sort of like a big dumb teddy bear. And the scene with Jon wasn't all Luke's fault, either. I had never done anything to discourage him from thinking I was his girl.

But truthfully, Luke didn't interest me at all as a boyfriend. I didn't think the spark, or the chemistry, or whatever, would ever be there between us. But I kept thinking, *If you don't want an intellectual in your life, then this is the sort of guy you have to be content with. So shut up and be content!*

"C'mon, Luke," I said with a sigh. "Sit down if you want to. I'm sorry I got angry."

Except for the prom, the kids at Lincoln High wear jeans, sweaters, even T-shirts to dances. As informal as possible, that's the rule. It must be some kind of rebellion, a way of saying, "This is no big deal to *me*. I know this is nothing more than a bunch of records being played in the stupid old gymnasium."

So on Saturday night as I looked through my closet, I tried to decide whether to go with the crowd and wear my jeans or whether to be different and show up in a skirt. But if I wore something too fancy, Luke would think I was trying to impress him. I sure didn't want that.

Finally I double-checked the section of my closet where I kept my really wacky stuff. I settled on a skirt, but not an ordinary skirt. A picture of Captain Kirk from "Star Trek" peered out from the folds of the bright, metallic-blue material. It was an outrageous garment I'd picked up in a thrift shop downtown once, on an impulse.

I smiled. The skirt, along with a billowing white cotton blouse, would certainly be unusual.

I washed my hair until it squeaked, then brushed it until my scalp ached. I carefully put on just the right eye makeup, blush, and just a trace of lip gloss. I never admitted, even to myself, that I was making such a fuss because Jon Madison was going to be there with some unknown girl.

39

Luke came to the house to pick me up. He was pretty good with parents. For some reason he knew how to impress them. And I don't think my parents are naive. They just thought of Luke as a perfectly nice young man.

Bill, however, made a gagging gesture behind Luke's back whenever he had a chance. He had already talked to me about Luke, earlier, up in my room.

"Why are you wasting your time with a noodlehead like that?" he'd asked. "Kerry, I think you really underestimate yourself, you know that?"

"I do not. Luke is good-looking, and he's one of the most popular boys at school. So what if he's not smart? Everyone can't be brilliant, you know."

"Oh, give me a break. Luke Russell is about as interesting as mashed potatoes. Is that what you want from life—a diet of mashed potatoes?"

"I'm not going to go with Luke for *life*, for heaven's sake. This is just an ordinary dance. Someday I'll meet the right boy—a boy with sensitivity. Maybe an artist."

I had paused to lift my puppy, who had come back from the hospital, up onto my bed. "Mmmm, yes, that's who I'd like to meet, an

40

artistic boy with the sensitivity to understand all my problems with my photography career."

Bill had looked as though he wanted to tear his hair out by the roots. "An artist. Egad. Well, at least that would be better than Luke, the Big *Duh*."

We said our goodbyes to my parents, and Dad told Luke to drive carefully, as he did every single time we went out. Then we went to pick up Cindy and Phil. Cindy looked great in her new tan blouse and a pair of jeans. Cindy was small and sort of exotic-looking, with dark hair and big dark eyes. Phil was kind of short, too, but solid enough to be a good football player. They made a cute couple.

"Wow, Kerry, you really put on lots of makeup," Cindy said right away, which I thought was very tactless of her. "I'm glad we're getting there early," she added. "We can grab a table so that a bunch of us have a place to sit."

The Sadie Hawkins Dance was a little different from most of the school dances because the entertainment committee decorated the gym to give it a hillbilly sort of atmosphere— stalks of corn, piles of pumpkins, hay, and a fake shack that was supposed to look like Li'l Abner's mountaintop home. And the DJ tried to sound like a real down-home country boy. Otherwise, it was the same old stuff.

Luke was really in the spirit of things. He wanted to dance every dance, fast and slow. I just wasn't that energetic, but I tried to keep up with him.

After one slow dance, we went back to find that a new couple had taken the seats at the end of our table—Jon and his date, Claudia Martin. She was another one of the super-brains. A math whiz, Claudia was known for being president of the Math Club and a top scorer on the math team.

So, I thought, *this is the kind of girl Jon goes for.*

Suddenly I felt depressed. It was as though someone had turned down all the lights and there was a gray shadow over the whole dumb dance. Nothing was fun any more, and I became very angry with myself for feeling that way.

Grow up, Kerry, I snapped at myself. What had I expected, anyway? A boy as good-looking as Jon wasn't going to sit around at home like some kind of hermit. Why should he? And he and Claudia probably had lots in common: math and computers and the high honor roll.

And chess? I wondered if Claudia played chess, too.

I stared down the long table at her and wished that she wore glasses or had big feet or something. But she was really sort of pretty. If I had to find a fault, it would be that she dressed a little too casually. Even though everyone wore jeans, Claudia's were baggier and older, and she had on a faded yellow sweatshirt. Of course, I was wearing my "Star Trek" skirt and standing out like a three-piece suit at a punk-rock concert.

"Hey, Kerry," Luke yelled out in his usual loud voice. "I think they're playing our song."

"What's our song?"

"You know, that Billy Joel song." Luke tugged at me to get up and dance again.

Well, why not? I decided. There was no sense giving in to a feeling of depression, especially when I had absolutely no reason for it. I might as well enjoy the dance.

As I stood up, I thought I saw Jon watching Luke and me. He was probably thinking what a loudmouth Luke was. But I didn't have time to dwell on it because Luke announced to the whole world that we were about to dance to "our song," and we whirled off toward the middle of the gym floor.

Luke embarrasses me, I thought, my face flaming red. I wondered just why I was there with such a clown, good-looking or not. I decided right then that I would rather spend Saturday nights at home, alone, than be out with Luke Russell.

I looked past Luke's shoulder and caught a glimpse of Jon dancing with Claudia. My stomach got all knotted up. Jon looked as though he was having a good time. I knew I should be glad for him. After all, he was a nice guy.

But I was definitely not glad for him.

Chapter Five

"Did you have a good time at the dance?" I spoke with extreme formality on Monday morning when I went to hand Bill's chess move to Jon.

He was at his locker, fiddling with the combination, and he turned, surprised to see me. "Oh. Kerry, hi. I'm sorry, what did you ask me? I was busy working the combination—"

"Oh, nothing much. Just wondered if you had fun at the dance. Here's the chess move." I sort of shoved it at him.

Jon stopped to study me, and there was a funny half-smile on his face. "It was a decent dance," he said quietly. "How about you? Have fun with Mr. Personality?"

"Oh, sure," I lied. But I felt that Jon somehow knew I was lying. He was smiling so knowingly. I went on quickly to say, "I suppose you and Claudia have been going out for a while now?"

"Going out?" He said the words as though he'd never heard them before. "No, I wouldn't say that. We're just friends from the Math Club. I was surprised when she invited me to the dance."

"Well, you never know, do you?" I said brightly. "Still waters run deep, they say."

"And what about noisy waters, Kerry?"

"What?"

He laughed. "I mean you. You're noisy waters, most of the time, but I have a feeling that there's more to you than most people realize."

I looked right at him. It was hard to do, maybe because he had that kind of lean, intelligent face that was becoming so appealing to me. And I did not want to find Jon Madison appealing!

Our eyes met and held, and I felt my insides getting all nervous, the way they did every time I saw the sparkle in his soft gray eyes.

46

"Well, are you?" he persisted. "Are you deep, like still waters?"

"For heaven's sake! No." I said. "I told you already. My brother's got all the depth in our family. I'm just—just me, I guess."

Jon frowned, as though he was thinking things over. That was one trait I liked about him: he never seemed judgmental. He just accepted things as they were.

"OK, you have Bill's chess move," I said, winding up the conversation. "I have to get to class now."

" 'Bye, Kerry."

As I walked away, it seemed as though his eyes were still on me, all the way down the hall.

"How is the game going, anyway?"

I was standing near Bill's shoulder as he pored over the chessboard in the living room.

"I'm not sure. Jon is a good strategist. That last move he made, that queen sacrifice, really surprised me. But I guess I can recover."

"I hope so," I said, meaning it. "I mean, Jon is a nice guy and all, but we've got to uphold the honor of the Fields family."

Bill was rubbing his eyes. "I'm so tired. I've been studying for two days straight, and today was my exam." He looked up at me. "I could go for a movie tonight. How about you?"

"Of course. Always. What's playing?"

Bill lifted his eyebrows like Groucho Marx. "There's a great sci-fi film at the Palace in Midville. *The Fifty-Fourth Planet*. I think you'd like it."

"Sounds good to me." I loved going to the movies with my brother. First of all, he usually paid, and that was always a help, especially given the way I handled money. But mostly, I loved the way Bill interpreted films. Of course, whatever movie we went to see, usually Bill has read about it first, so he was always miles ahead of me.

We arrived at the Palace about ten minutes before the show started.

"I suppose you plan to stuff yourself with popcorn as usual," Bill said, rummaging in his pockets for some change.

"Absolutely not," I answered, but he went over to buy a giant container, anyway. He knew I wouldn't be able to resist having some, with lots of hot, melted butter.

"So. Is that your brother, or are you dating someone behind Luke's back?" asked a voice from behind me. It was Jon.

"Hi. And, yes, that's my brother." I turned to see if Jon was alone. He was. No Claudia.

Bill came back, and Jon greeted him like a

long-lost friend. "Hey, Bill. I've been hoping to get a chance to meet you! I'm Jon Madison."

Bill pushed the popcorn bucket at me so that he could give Jon a good hearty hand-shake. You would have thought it was reunion week, the way those two crowed about "meet-ing at last." I guess they had really come to respect each other since they had started the chess game.

"So what are you doing here?" Bill asked. "You a sci-fi freak, too?"

"Are you kidding?" Jon gave a self-con-scious sort of laugh. "I've read this guy's book at least four times. No way I was going to miss the movie."

"Me neither. I read all his stuff. So listen, why don't you sit with us? We can compare notes. I want to be sure I don't miss a thing."

I felt out of it. I, of course, had never read the book. I felt a little like taking the popcorn and sitting somewhere off in a corner, all by myself. But of course I didn't. I trotted along behind the two geniuses and somehow ended up sitting between the two of them.

"Have some popcorn, guys," I said in a cheerful voice, but they didn't even hear me. They were busy gabbing about the movie, the book, and all the other books they'd read by the same author. Actually, the picture was

49

pretty good. But I kept thinking about how much simpler it would have been if I'd gone to see something like *The Tomato Plant That Gobbled Up Hoboken* with Cindy.

"I'm glad we finally met, Jon," Bill said after the movie had ended. "Listen. I was wondering if you have time for a face-to-face chess game some night this week?"

Jon looked pleased. "Any night you want."

So they settled on Wednesday night, at our house.

Well, I certainly won't be there, I decided firmly. As nice as Jon was, I didn't want to get to know him any better. That would only lead to trouble; he'd find out how unintellectual I was, and that would be that.

But it had been hard sitting next to him in the theater. I had been so aware of him that I'd flinched whenever he'd slipped his arm on the armrest between us. I was even conscious of the way Jon smelled, which was clean and masculine—and nice.

I did not like feeling inferior, that's what it all boiled down to. My whole life I'd been hearing, "Well, Kerry, are you as smart as your brother?" from teachers. And even in our family, relatives had a habit of comparing me to Bill. "My, Kerry certainly is nothing like Bill, is

50

she?" they'd say. "I suppose she's more the sociable type, rather than the scholarly type."

Who needed that? I can even remember my two grandmothers talking about me, years ago. "It's lucky that Kerry is such a little beauty, with those big eyes and the strawberry hair. She'll be able to land a nice, smart husband and never have to worry."

From my own grandmothers! I had made up my mind, even way back then, that I'd never try to "land" a husband, especially a smart one. I'd learn to make my way in life alone, on my own.

It was raining when we came out of the theater, big, fat drops, and there was a wind. Bill asked Jon if he wanted to go to the diner for coffee with us.

"Thanks, but no," he said. "I still have a lot of homework to do in chemistry and English."

"English?" I echoed. "I didn't know we had any English homework."

"Sure. You know that vocabulary list Mr. Bandero assigned. He's going to test us on it tomorrow."

"Oh, no!" I gasped.

"Cheer up. It's only twenty words."

"Yeah, but what words! *Nebulous* and *credulous* and *magniloquent* and *sententious*—"

Bill laughed. "I always loved those high-school vocab lessons. How about *'Laggard is to procrastinate as arbiter is to adjudicate'*? That one always comes in handy."

"Thanks a bunch." I groaned.

"You can do it, Kerry," Jon said. "Or would you—no, I suppose you wouldn't—"

"What?"

"I was going to say, I could help you study for English, if you want."

Immediately I felt defensive. If he'd asked me anything else, it would have been different. But offering to help me study? My inferiority complex flared up and made me stubborn.

"I really don't need anyone's help," I said politely. "But thank you, anyway."

"I figured that. Well, good luck." Jon smiled and patted my arm in encouragement. "Maybe you'd better skip coffee and do some cramming tonight."

"That's right. That's just what she'll do," Bill said firmly. "Well, good meeting you, Jon. See you on Wednesday."

So like a good little girl, I went on home with Bill to learn the definitions of *nebulous* and *credulous* and *magniloquent* and *sententious*.

But I kept thinking about Jon and the way he had patted my arm. Why did I have to be so affected by that boy, when I didn't want to be?

52

Chapter Six

The next day I went back to my usual craziness. Camera in hand, I stalked the corridors of Lincoln High for yearbook photos, not caring how my hair looked or even if my shirt was on wrong. Though luckily it wasn't.

I wanted to be on the alert for a really good picture for the statewide contest. Besides, I had promised the yearbook editor a batch of unusual school shots, and that's what I would deliver.

All morning I sneaked up on people, mostly seniors and teachers, and before they could notice I was there, I snapped their pictures. Nobody minded, not even the couple who was kissing in an out-of-the-way corner of the building when they should have been hurrying off to class.

Kerry the Flash was back in action.

During a free period, which I usually used as a study hall, I tiptoed toward the computer room, hoping to surprise Ms. Klein, the popular math teacher who was usually there. She wasn't in the room, but Jon was. And he didn't see me.

Oh, well, he was a senior, too, I thought. I adjusted my lens and zoomed in on him as he sat there, unsuspecting, bent over a mile-long printout. The morning sun was slanting warmly into the room. With the filtered light and the computer screens, it would make an interesting photo. I snapped the picture.

Jon didn't yell out, "Hey, what are you doing?" the way everyone else did before they began to laugh. He just looked up and smiled a friendly greeting.

"Hey. That's a Robert Redford smile you've got there," I said impulsively and took another quick photo. "Hope you don't mind seeing yourself in the yearbook, Jon."

"Not at all," he answered cheerfully. "You can even put me down as Official Class Nerd, if you want. I guess I look like it, with this printout."

I frowned and lowered my camera. "You're not the class nerd. You're not a nerd at all. I told you before, you should be *proud* of being intelligent. Bill's as smart as you are, and doing really well at Polytech."

"Thanks, Kerry. I'll try to remember that." But his face had clouded over, and he had turned off. He went back to his intense inspection of the printout.

What's wrong with him today? I wondered. Shrugging, I packed my equipment into the camera bag and left without even saying goodbye.

On Wednesday night, I was still determined to stay far away from the chess game between Bill and Jon. I'd had enough of feeling stupid at the movies, so I decided I'd keep really busy and avoid seeing Jon altogether.

At dinner I told my mother I'd do the dishes and that I'd even mop the kitchen floor. Mom looked thrilled.

"The girl is losing her mind," my dad said, staring at me across the dining room table. "*Offering* to do dishes and housework?"

"I think it's very kind of Kerry," my mother said defensively. "Maybe she's finally decided to help her mother around the house."

Bill almost choked on his spaghetti. "Kerry?

You've got to be joking if you think she's interested in being some kind of Betty Crocker."

"I am not joking." My mother gave him a puzzled look. "Every girl, sooner or later, wants to learn to keep a nice home."

"Yeah, especially your daughter Kerry," Bill said, chuckling. "Next thing you know, she'll be baking apple strudels and learning how to make a pot roast."

Poor Mom looked confused. "I don't see why not, Bill. If Kerry hopes to marry a nice young man some day . . . ."

Oh, no. I'd heard that one before, from my grandmothers. I decided it would be easier just to change the subject.

"Bill's having company tonight for a chess game," I told them. "I imagine he'll be using the living room."

"Fine. No problem." Dad looked up from his forkful of meat. "We were planning to watch TV in the den, anyway."

"And I'll be developing pictures after I do the kitchen," I announced.

The previous summer Bill and Dad had built me a small darkroom in the basement. I had all the chemicals I needed to do developing on my own, as well as an enlarger and a built-in sink.

I was pleased that I had the whole evening

planned out so that I wouldn't have to think about Jon Madison being in our house.

But all that changed when I printed my photographs.

There I was, sloshing the paper around in the developer, even whistling a little tune and feeling like a real professional photographer. I hummed as I hung up the prints, one by one, and visualized myself as a happy career woman, busy and successful.

Suddenly I came across the pictures I'd taken of Jon in the computer room. As they darkened in the developer tray, I stared at the prints and felt a growing mixture of fear and excitement.

Even in the glow of the red safety light, I could see that the computer room pictures had come out just as I had imagined. The sunlight slanting in across Jon's face made every lean line in his profile stand out. He looked intelligent, for one thing, but he also looked warm and human and—so lovable.

What was *wrong* with me, anyway? So what if he looked lovable? Let someone else love him! Claudia, for instance.

I tried to toughen myself against my feelings. As I moved the first print into the fixer, I put the second print into the developer tray. It was the one of Jon smiling. Correction. Jon smiling at *me*.

It was Jon's smile that finished me off. Suddenly I knew, without doubt, that I was falling in love with him. And that was absolutely crazy! Of all the people in this world, he was the last one I wanted to fall in love with.

I was hypnotized by the two pictures, but especially by the smiling one. I could swear that that smile was just for me, as though he thought I was someone special. What had he said that morning? I tried to remember, but my mind was too confused to recall.

Still, the evidence was there, in black and white. Jon had smiled at me as though I were the only girl in the whole wide world.

Was it possible? Could he feel something for me? It certainly didn't seem likely, not when he had someone like Claudia Martin chasing after him. And with all of their common interests—the Math Club, the Computer Club—it would be easy for her.

And me? I was apt to be under a desk or buried in puppies. I was always late to class and unprepared with the homework—things he couldn't possibly comprehend. *No. I must be reading the picture wrong. He can't care for me!*

So I looked again. I was getting pretty good

at photography by now, and also good at interpreting what my camera recorded. And I didn't need a psychology degree to interpret what I saw there: Jon's face was lit up just for me.

But that was only half the problem. The other half was that there *I* was, standing in my darkroom with my heart pounding and my whole body shot full of adrenaline just because I had suddenly remembered that Jon Madison was going to be in my house that night! In fact, no doubt he was there already. I'd been hiding out in the darkroom for over an hour.

I love him, I thought in wonder. *I don't want to, but I really do love him.*

And why? Was it because he was so smart, or was it in spite of his being so smart? Was it because he was so cheerful and because he never seemed to look down on me for being scatterbrained? I had no idea.

In a daze, I cleaned up the darkroom. I wanted to go upstairs and be in the same room as Jon. I wanted to see if I was imagining things or if I was really in love.

There's such a thing as puppy love, too, I reminded myself.

That could be it. I might just have a small, silly crush on the guy, and in a week or two it would be gone, sort of like a bad cold. I hoped that was it. I finished straightening things up and took one more look at Jon's photos as they hung on my little line. Then I went upstairs to join the guys in the living room.

There, across the chessboard from Bill, sat the object of my newly discovered love. He looked great. He was wearing a white button-down shirt and a nice pair of jeans. He'd had his hair trimmed, and it fell in a mass of soft, dark curls. His face was lean and intense.

As I walked into the room, Bill threw out a "Hi, Kerry," without looking up. Jon did the same. They were really into their game. Even so, I thought, they could have at least looked up for one second!

"Hate to say it, Kerry," Bill said, "but you don't smell too good."

Oh, my gosh! I thought, horrified. I'd forgotten how awful the darkroom chemicals smelled! I rushed upstairs to take the quickest shower in history.

Then, smelling as sweet as a spring flower, I went back to the living room and wandered casually over to the boys. "How's it going?" I asked.

Neither of them answered.

"Really intense, hmmm?" I offered.

Silence. Their eyes were glued to the board. Their fingers were in fast motion, moving the chess pieces quicker than I'd ever seen anyone do. I wondered what was going on.

"Check," said Bill, and then he said quickly to me, "Sorry, Kerry, but this is a lightning game."

What in blazes is a lightning game? I wondered.

"Forget check," said Jon. "Did you overlook my bishop?"

Bill groaned. Jon chuckled. I stood there, feeling foolish, and stared down at Jon's hair and shoulders and the straight line of his spine.

You're a jerk, Kerry, a real jerk, I thought. *He doesn't even know you're alive!*

But I wasn't leaving. I decided to perch myself on a chair so I could watch the game. Maybe if I showed a lot of interest, they'd include me in on things. So I sat there and watched. But neither of them said a word to me.

A lightning game, I learned later, is one that's timed. The limit is usually ten minutes. The players are challenged to move their pieces quickly and try to win before the ten minutes are up.

It seemed like just my luck to come along and try to get Jon's attention when he was involved in a lightning game!

My luck didn't get much better when they started the next game, either. It was a conventional, long game of chess. I brought Jon and Bill glasses of soda, and I even put a bowl of peanuts beside them. They drank the soda and munched on the peanuts like starving prisoners, but they never looked my way.

"So, what's going on, anyway?" I asked once, trying to sound feminine and intelligent and very, very interested.

Silence. Then Bill said, "You wouldn't understand, Kerry." Jon said nothing. I didn't exist, apparently, during this critical game.

Fine, I thought at last. I knew when I wasn't wanted. I could always go and watch TV with my parents.

But I didn't. I curled up on the couch with a photography magazine, simply because I wanted to stay in the same room as Jon. *If this is what love is like,* I thought, *I wish I could switch it off the way you switch off a stereo set.*

Hours later, Bill finally won. I knew it was over because I heard Bill say, "Check," and then, a short while after, "Mate." I hoped that, with the game over, Jon would look at me and smile the way he had in the photograph. My hopes fell when I realized they were already immersed in conversation.

The two of them had a zillion things to talk about: chess games, computers, the Polytech campus, the financial-aid program at the college. The list seemed endless. I found myself gritting my teeth and wishing I could squirt them both with a water gun. If only I'd had a water gun!

Then Jon got ready to leave.

"So, listen, you'll put me down for the human chess game, won't you, Bill?" he asked. "That's something I'd hate to miss."

My ears perked up. "What are you talking about?" I blurted out. "What human chess game?"

"You know, Kerry. The game we have every year at school," Bill said. "Well, maybe I never mentioned it to you before, but it's a big event at Polytech."

I sat up straighter and threw down the magazine. "You mean people pretend to be chess pieces?"

"That's it." Bill grinned. "I don't think you'd be interested in it. Except for the costumes, maybe, which are sensational. But Jon wants to be in it, so I'll sign him up to play."

"I'd like to be in it, too, Bill," I said quickly, surprising even myself.

"*You*, Kerry? You've never had any interest—"

"There comes a time when a person must broaden her horizons," I said firmly. "After all, I'll be in college next year, too, and I'd like to see what campus activities are all about."

"Good idea." Jon was nodding his head as though he approved. But he wasn't giving me that dazzling smile that I'd been waiting all evening to see.

Bill shook his head in confusion. "Well, sure, if you want to be in it, we always need players. I'll put your name down on the list, too."

Bill really looked puzzled. But Jon didn't seem to notice as he shook hands with Bill and said what a great evening it had been and how he'd loved the competitive games.

Say something to me, I thought, my heart beating wildly from Jon's nearness.

"G'night, Kerry. Thanks for the soda and peanuts."

I watched him put on his jacket and leave.

Chapter Seven

Once I started to believe I was in love, I was constantly on the lookout for Jon—in school, after school, anywhere that I might be able to spot him.

But if I'd thought it was going to be easy, I was very wrong. It would have been easier to set my sights on that year's Nobel Prize—in anything!

He wasn't in any of my classes except English, because he took mostly those high-level courses. I was in the middle with the average students.

So it required planning to try to catch Jon. I knew where his locker was, so I made little detours to pass by it. If I saw him, I'd pull myself together and then casually stroll over and say hi. At least every other day, I had the excuse of giving him Bill's chess move, since they were still playing their original correspondence game. He, too, would come looking for me to give me back his move.

And that's where things began to go wrong.

One day, he found me sitting outside the principal's office. "Looks like you're in some kind of trouble, Kerry," he asked with concern. "Anything bad?"

"Oh, no," I insisted, sitting up taller in the chair and trying to look perfectly innocent. "No, I'm not in trouble. I'm here to see Mr. Farber about, er, about a series of photos for the—um—yearbook."

Just then Mr. Farber's secretary came to call me. "All right, Miss Fields. You may go in. And maybe now you can explain to Mr. Farber exactly why you were out on that fire escape, camera or no camera!"

Jon started laughing, but not in a mean way. He winked at me as if to say "Good luck," then headed down the hall. I absolutely melted at the thought of his winking one of those eyes at me. It was what sustained me throughout the scolding I received from Mr. Farber. I hadn't thought going out on the fire escape to get a few candid shots for the yearbook would cause such a stir. I also hadn't planned on getting caught.

Then there was the time Jon was coming along the hall with Claudia at his side. She was walking fast, trying to keep up with his long-legged stride, and she was talking nonstop about the upcoming match the Math Club was having against North High School.

Under my breath I said, "Hmmmph."

Jon stopped when he saw me by my locker. "Excuse me for a moment, Claudia. Kerry, here's my chess move." He handed me the usual small piece of paper. Claudia was glaring daggers at me, so I decided to give her something to worry about.

"Why, thank you, Jon." My voice was dripping sweetness. "And I certainly hope you'll be coming over to our house again soon."

That really got to Claudia. She looked furious!

"My goodness, Kerry," she said, her voice just as sickeningly sweet as mine had been. "Who is that you have taped inside your locker? Ugh, it looks like some kind of punk-rock star."

It was. My favorite rock star had played a concert nearby the year before. And of course I'd taken photos of him after the concert. He was really handsome, and I'd put the photo on my locker door to impress my girlfriends. But now it sure looked childish with brainy Jon and brainy Claudia standing there.

She had succeeded in making me look like a juvenile and a stupid groupie. But I didn't have to take it lying down.

"I have his picture there because it's such a good photograph, Claudia," I answered deftly. "Even Mr. Shannon mentioned that this was a perfect example of panning. You know, blurring the background with a clear, moving subject." I smiled.

"Wow," Jon said, moving closer to take a look. "Mr. Shannon said that?" Naturally he was impressed by whatever Mr. Shannon, the calculus expert, said about anything. "He's right, Kerry. The photo has great composition."

It's not as good as the one I have of you, Jon, I thought.

I managed to look humble. His praise warmed me, and it was nice to realize that I'd gotten back at Claudia, just a little bit.

But on Friday afternoon I really pulled a Kerry "special."

I had cleanup duty at the animal hospital, and my job included taking some of the healthier dogs out for walks in the field behind the clinic. I was rushing around, with a million chores still to finish, and it seemed like a good idea to take a bunch of dogs out there and get their walks over with all at once.

I was walking five dogs at the same time when a VW Rabbit pulled into the clinic parking lot. I didn't recognize the car, but panic rose in me when I thought I saw Jon get out of it. It was him all right, and he was looking for me to give me his chess move!

I tried to hide behind the building, but it was no use. I heard Dr. Turner at the door saying, "Kerry? Yes, she's here today. I'm sure she's around the back with one of the dogs."

I wanted to flatten myself against the wall and never be seen again. Jon, however, came searching for me and there was no place to hide.

The German shepherd was charging toward his favorite tree. The two little poodles were winding around me as though I were a flagpole. The terrier was barking because it wanted to run, and the big, tan mutt, who was named Elvis, was jumping up trying to lick my face.

Bravely, I stepped forward to greet Jon as though nothing were wrong.

He stopped dead. His eyebrows went up.

"Haven't I seen this movie before?" he said.

"I mean, the one with you, and more dogs than you can handle?"

"Ha-ha," I said clearly. "Very funny. This is part of my job, you know. Even sick animals need a break from their cages, after all."

"But five of them?" He scratched his head. He really looked adorable when he did that. The great genius looking totally befuddled. "Five of them all at once?"

I tried to look unconcerned. "No problem." I yanked on the leashes and tried to bring the dogs back into line. It didn't work. Elvis, the mutt, had decided to chase the poodles, and the German shepherd began barking at Jon. It was terrible.

Jon just stood there looking at me. I couldn't read the expression on his face. It could have been anything from amusement to admiration—to stark terror.

Finally he said just one thing. "You really are something, Kerry." And he tried to give me the piece of paper with his chess move. "I forgot to give you this at school."

"I don't really have a free hand, Jon," I explained as reasonably as I could.

"Oh, of course not. I'm sorry, Kerry." He turned a bit red. "I really am a space cadet. Here, let me help you."

Jon took the leashes of three of the dogs. They started to pull him every which way.

"I don't know, Kerry. This doesn't seem to be helping you any." The dogs had their leashes wrapped around his long legs in record time. He was losing his balance as he tried to hand me his chess move.

"It's all right," I said quickly. "Just give me the paper."

Somehow he handed me his chess move, and I was able to tuck it into the back pocket of my jeans.

"You certainly live a dangerous life," he commented, a little out of breath from the exertion of trying to control the three dogs going in different directions.

I felt overwhelmed with embarrassment. Why *did* I live my life in such a crazy, whirlwind way?

"Can I help you take them back inside?" Jon asked, but I could tell that he was eager to get away.

"No. No problem," I smiled graciously. "This is my job, and I can handle them all."

"If you say so." He handed back the leashes. "I think you're the bravest girl I've ever known." He was shaking his head with disbelief.

The stupidest, you mean, I thought.

71

"I've got to get going to my own job," Jon said.

"You never told me. Where do you work?"

"I work a few afternoons a week at Comptronics. It's a small mail-order computer company over on South Street." He paused. "It's pretty dull, compared to your job. Well, I'll see you, Kerry."

"Sure," I said sadly. "I'll see you."

When he was gone, I moaned out loud.

"Oh, Elvis," I wailed to the barking mutt. "Would you believe it? I think I've managed to do it again!"

Chapter Eight

The day of the human chess game, a Sunday, finally arrived. Jon and Bill were excited because they loved the "royal game" as they called chess. *I* was excited because I would have a chance to be with Jon for the better part of an afternoon.

Maybe I could find some way to make him notice me—as a girl, and not just as Bill's sister.

"This is so great," Jon said when we picked him up at his house. "I really want to thank you for inviting me, Bill."

"Hey, the Chess Club is glad you could make it. As I said, we're always looking for players."

I was interested in where Jon lived. His house was a lot like ours, a modest, two-story, oldish type on a street that had been established years ago, when the city was young. As our street, Jon's had tall oak trees and plenty of shade. It looked like a nice place for a kid to grow up.

I found myself wishing I'd known Jon when he was a kid. I wondered if he had been cute back then, too, and if he had been as smart and had spent much of his early life reading and studying, the way Bill had.

Oh, he was *not* the right boy for me to love, I knew that. I knew it so well. But how could I tell my heart to stop pounding every time I looked at him?

In a lighthearted mood, we drove out to the Polytech campus.

"I have to remind you—mostly you, Kerry," Bill said as he pulled into the parking lot near the student union building. "This human chess game is serious business. The Chess Club sponsors it, and we take the game pretty seriously. So even though people are in strange costumes, please don't pull any of your crazy stunts."

"I wouldn't." I was indignant when both Bill and Jon began to chuckle. "Well, I wouldn't!" I insisted. "I mean, I did bring my camera, but

74

that's only in case there's anything really fabulous to photograph."

Both boys groaned. "Her camera," Bill said fearfully. "I wonder if you have any idea, Jon, of the stunts this girl can pull in the interest of photographic art?"

Jon's face lit up. "I think I do have some small sense of it, yes." And they both laughed again.

"Just try to restrain yourself, OK, Kerry? I mean, I still have another year here after this one. If you embarrass me, I might have to leave town."

But I knew Bill was only teasing me. He was never terribly bothered by the things I did. With Jon, however, I couldn't be too sure. So I promised to behave like a perfect lady.

We walked across the campus, savoring the beautiful, early autumn day. The weather was unseasonably warm, and the bright blue sky was dotted with fluffy clouds. We didn't even need our sweaters.

I was wearing my best outfit: a turquoise pullover blouse and a trim pair of navy pants that were very flattering. Cindy had helped me choose what to wear.

"You can't wear a skirt," she had told me. "You don't even know what you'll be *doing* in that chess game. The whole thing sounds crazy to me, anyway!" Cindy just couldn't understand my sudden obsession with a game of chess at the college.

"Here it is," Bill announced as we turned the corner around the Polytech field house. And there, stretched out on a long, green playing field, was the most gigantic chessboard I had ever seen. It was amazing.

Jon and I both gasped. The board was about fifty feet long by fifty feet wide and had been constructed out of squares of cloth secured at the corners. Some of the squares were white, the others black, so they formed a perfect chessboard.

There were banners hung about, fluttering from poles and giving the whole scene a festive medieval look. I heard music, flutes and harps, lutes and lyres, the kind of music that would have been playing if it really had been the Middle Ages.

"But who sets all this up?" I asked, knowing that the Chess Club wasn't quite this imaginative.

"There's a group on campus that provides the costumes and medieval pomp," Bill told me. "A club known as the AMR—the Association for Medieval Remembrance."

"I've heard about them." Jon sounded really impressed. "They spend their weekends having jousts and tournaments and feasts. They really get into it."

"But the *costumes*," I said. "They're just spectacular!" And they were. I saw students walking around dressed as knights, in shining armor, and bishops. with big, padded bellies and clerical robes. I spotted a rook, a student made up to look like a castle, and he really did, too.

"Wow—look at the kings and queens!" Jon pointed as the royal assembly came sweeping across the field toward the chessboard. The white king and queen, dressed in sparkling white satin, walked beside the black king and queen, who were, of course, all in black. Their crowns glittered in the sunlight. All four moved sedately, quite royally, toward their correct squares on the chessboard.

"It's fantastic," I said. "I've never seen anything like it!"

"It is really amazing, isn't it?" Jon was staring down at me suddenly, looking amused because I was so enthusiastic. "I'll bet you never knew chess could be this exciting, did you, Kerry?"

"Nope." My cheeks felt suddenly warm because Jon was looking at me so intently.

"Chess is a neat game." Jon turned away and looked out across the giant board as more people arrived. He was squinting in the sun. "In chess there are always at least two things happening at once. You have to keep your eye on the game, or else you might miss something important."

I blinked. The way Jon had said that, it seemed as though he was talking about something else besides chess. *But what? What did he mean by more than two things happening at once?* What was he referring to?

I wished I were smart, like Bill and Jon! I wished so much that I could follow everything they were saying all the time and understand the obscure, deep things they said.

I felt a bit lost for a moment. How could I ever hope to impress someone like Jon Madison? I must have been insane to let myself fall for him. *Oh, well,* I thought, stealing a glance at him, *it's nice just being with Jon, and loving him secretly, even if nothing ever comes of it!*

The music whipped up to a fanfare as more of the players came marching out toward the giant chessboard. Each costume was as impressive as the one before it.

And suddenly I realized that I had something more important than love to think about; I had to get a picture portfolio of the event. That chess game might be my winning entry in the photography contest, if I could do it right.

I looked around furtively. The best angle for photos, I knew, would be from up high somewhere. Right away, I spotted a tree that would be perfect. It was a high maple just off to the side of the chessboard's midpoint. It was loaded with sturdy branches, and it looked easy to climb.

Of course, climbing that tree would be pulling what Bill called one of my crazy stunts, and I knew that he'd probably disapprove.

While I was still thinking, Bill herded Jon and me over to a costume table that was set up just inside a striped tent.

"You two will need costumes right away," Bill said. "Looks like we're short a few players." Bill would be working with the sound system, controlling the microphone for the club members who would be calling out the chess moves.

Still hugging my camera bag to my side, I waited to see what sort of costume I'd get. Of course I was hoping for something beautiful and devastatingly feminine, something that would knock Jon right off his feet.

But they made me a pawn.

"Are you *kidding*?" I wailed when the costume girl handed me a costume of black burlap that looked like a pile of old rags. "Why do I have to be a pawn?"

"Because pawns are the most needed, Kerry," Bill whispered to me in a please-be-reasonable tone of voice. Jon, on the other hand, was being outfitted as a knight. Wouldn't you just know it? He looked dashing and royally handsome, and I looked plain and ugly.

Grumbling and mumbling, I slipped into my burlap. Oh, boy. There was a floppy hat that covered almost my whole face, and a pair of weird pointed cloth shoes. I was instructed to tie a thick rope around my waist, too.

"How to look gorgeous and glamorous in three easy steps," I muttered, plopping the idiotic hat on my head.

Jon heard me and laughed. "You look fine, Kerry. After all, there aren't many other female figures in chess."

"Sexism at its worst," I said, loud enough to embarrass Bill, who was working with the electricity by then. *Claudia wouldn't be seen in a getup like this, I'll bet,* I was thinking bitterly.

"You've got to remember something, Kerry." Jon spoke gently, in an instructional tone.

"One should never underestimate the power of a humble pawn."

I looked up at him. "You said that once before. What do you mean?"

"I mean that you must always remember that if a pawn reaches the other side of the board, which is entirely possible, then it becomes a queen."

I brightened at that. "Yeah? Really?"

"Really," he assured me.

At least there was hope, then. So I accepted my role as a pawn and clumped out there, in my cloth shoes, toward the square assigned to me. Jon and I were both on the black side, at least. That made it sort of cozy.

The game commenced at exactly two o'clock. A large crowd had turned out to see the festivities, mostly people who really took chess quite seriously. Personally, I thought the game would have been more fun if they had allowed the players to clown around a little, but that just wasn't done.

"The game of kings" was certainly a revered one in most circles. I looked over at Jon. He looked happier than I'd ever seen him, including at school. He was in his element at Polytech. He was with brilliant people who had the same interests as he had, especially chess, and he was having a wonderful time.

I wish I didn't love somebody like that, I thought, as I lumbered from square to square in my burlap. *I mean, let's face it, I really am a peasant pawn, and Jon really is sort of a knight in shining armor.*

But that kind of negative thinking is not my style, as a rule. So I tried to concentrate on something else—getting up the maple tree to take pictures.

They had told us we'd have to find a substitute if we needed to leave the board for any reason. I began to look around at the audience. And lo and behold, there was a young girl dressed in black clothes standing not too far away from my square.

"Pssst!" I tried to catch her eye. She heard me and moved closer. "Hey, listen, would you like to substitute for me for a little bit?"

The girl, who was no more than twelve said, "I'd *love* to have a chance to be out there! I even came dressed in black just hoping."

"Oh, great," I smiled happily.

"Sure. If you have to go to the bathroom, you just go right ahead. I'll substitute for you. Take as long as you want."

I slipped away quietly and went for my camera, then headed for the maple tree.

Oh, Kerry, I thought. *Don't mess up this time! Bill will never forgive you.*

It had sounded so easy. Just climb the tree and snap the pictures. But in reality, you have to be part monkey to get up the first few feet of a tree, before the first branch.

I scrambled several times until I made it to the branch. But from there on it was easy. And best of all, no one noticed me. So I kept on climbing until I found the best spot for a good, clear view.

It was great up there. I was hidden from view by the leaves, which had begun to turn colors but hadn't started falling off yet. And the panorama that was spread out before me was just incredible! I had a bird's-eye view of the human chess game, and that, I decided, was the only way to see the game.

I worked quickly with the camera, adjusting and focusing, then finally snapping. I zoomed in on the kings and queens especially, because they were doing a great acting job out there, being so coldly regal. And I snapped a few pictures of Jon, of course, because he was my special knight.

But all the characters were wonderful, so I kept on taking pictures until I'd run out of film. I was just getting ready to climb down when my hat fell off, plopping right onto the chessboard.

Chapter Nine

"What is that person doing up there?" a player shrieked. It was the white queen, no less, upon whose crown my hat had landed. She looked incredibly annoyed as well as quite silly with my limp felt hat dangling off one jeweled tip of her beautiful crown. She seemed determined to create a real fuss.

"This is crazy," the girl bellowed. "Why is there a pawn climbing around up in a tree?"

Everybody looked up at me, and I knew I was in big trouble.

"Off with her head!" I shouted, beyond caring. I began to slither down the tree, holding on tight to my precious photography equipment.

The people on the chessboard looked startled, and for a moment they just stared at each other, or else at me, the court jester descending in disgrace.

"Did she say 'Off with her head'?" asked the black queen. She was stifling a giggle. "That sounds like something out of *Alice in Wonderland!*"

The white king suddenly began to laugh. He was followed by several of the knights, and then there was a chorus of chuckles from somewhere else. Pretty soon the whole cast of characters, except for the sputtering white queen, was roaring with laughter.

And the crowd began to clap, too. *Oh, great,* I thought, *now Bill and his sedate Chess Club members will really hate me.*

But I was wrong. When I looked over at Bill, he was chuckling also, as were the rest of the moderators of the game. I slumped with relief.

"You're crazy. Funny, but crazy," a white bishop said to me after I had stowed my camera equipment along the sideline, and had slipped back into the game.

The black king, who was nearby, smiled at me and called out, "Hey, you sure shook up these stuffy people, and that's just what they needed."

So it really was all right. I'd gotten my photographs, and I'd been forgiven by the crowd. The little girl who'd been my substitute slapped me five and said she was proud of me. Then she hurried off.

And Jon, my lovable, dark-haired knight in all his finery, called out to me, "Way to go, Kerry." The visor of his helmet was down, for the moment, hiding his face from me, but I was sure that he was grinning.

The game finally got back to normal. It was rather slow-moving at times, but I loved it when I had the chance to be near my knight. I was so busy staring at him that I didn't even notice that my chess piece was moving, steadily and surely, toward the far end of the board.

"Looks like you might make it to the end," Jon told me at one point, giving me a conspiratorial wink.

All right, I thought. *Royalty, here I come!*

I waited patiently, thinking the whole time that those burlap clothes would have to go. I was eager to be dressed better so I could try out some serious flirting.

"Black pawn to D1," called out one of the

players over the loudspeaker. I jumped nearly a mile. That was me!

I had reached the other end. A smattering of applause was heard from the audience, especially the ones who, I imagined, remembered me as the clown from the tree.

"You are now a queen," I was told.

"Great," I answered. "Where's my new costume?"

He looked puzzled. "Oh, we don't usually—"

My hands flew to my hips. "What do you mean, you don't usually—? Don't give me that! I came a long way to get here, and I want to look like a queen. I want to act like a queen, and I plan to dress like a queen!"

There was laughter all around me, but I knew they were on my side. The white queen, I noticed, was sneering at me, but everyone else seemed to be my ally.

"Give the pawn her new costume," called out assorted voices. "Yeah, come on! She deserves to wear a queen's outfit!"

The crowd kept chanting until the members of the Chess Club finally gave in, looking exasperated. They halted the game and led me back to the costume tent, where I stripped off the pawn's burlap in no time at all.

"Here you go, Your Highness," said the costume girl, who was from the Association for

Medieval Remembrance. "We don't have another black dress, so this will have to do." Smiling, she chose for me a long gown of creamy, satiny gold, with a high neckline and a bodice of rich antique lace. "It will look sensational with your red hair!"

I loved that gown. It seemed to have been made just for me, and as I slipped into it, I felt happier than I had in a long time.

"I don't blame you for wanting a costume of your own," the girl from the AMR said. "Who would want to be a pawn forever?"

"Not me." I smiled at her as she finished off my ensemble with a sparkling, bejeweled crown, and a scepter. "Thanks so much. You don't know what you've done for me!" And then I sauntered back to the game, just as regally as anyone in the original royal party.

"You look beautiful, Kerry." Jon was the first one to speak when I stepped back onto the giant chessboard. "Hey, I told you you might make it, didn't I?"

"You sure did," I said, and gave him the most dazzling smile I possibly could. *What a flirt,* my friend Cindy would have said if she'd been there. And she would have been right.

I was outrageous for the rest of the game. I posed, and I showed off, and I sparkled, all in the direction of one special knight. It must have been obvious to everyone because at one point one of the pawns whispered to me, "If you don't capture that knight in this game, I'd say you're never going to."

I swished my long, voluminous skirt and threw another bright smile toward Jon, who was only a few squares away.

"Kerry, what do you say we stay on campus after this is over? If you feel like it, maybe we can even have dinner here."

Dinner? I couldn't believe he was asking me to stay with him for dinner.

"That sounds lovely," I said regally. "Do you mean with Bill, too?"

"No." Jon grinned at me mysteriously. "Bill told me he's planning to go home and study. Just you and me, if you don't mind taking the bus to get home."

Obviously I didn't mind. I'd have taken a dogsled through Siberia to be with Jon.

"I think that would be wonderful," I whispered.

So that's how we came to have a date that night. But later, as we continued to move around the chessboard, I began to wonder if Jon had asked me out only because I was so blatantly flirting.

The more I thought about it, the more sure I was that that was just what had happened.

He's only amused, I thought, *and in playing along with what he thinks is a game on my part.* That made my victory a little bit hollow, but not by much.

After all, a date was a date. And I was ready to settle for anything, as long as it meant being alone with Jon.

Before the game ended, I had the pleasure of watching the white queen, in all her glory, being taken off the board as she was captured.

"Too bad, dear," I murmured loud enough for her to hear me. She shot me a poisonous glance.

The rest of the game was a snap. The black team beat the white, in part because black had two queens—and one of them was me! I felt so important, and I was the first to lead the cheering when the final move was called.

After the game, I sadly changed back into my own clothes and went to meet Jon. As we walked into the restaurant, the Scavenger, I could see that it was not the place to go to be alone with a boy. The pub-style restaurant in the campus student union was filled with people—students, professors, and visitors like ourselves, who had come out to share in the festivities of the weekend.

But I didn't care. I was there with Jon, and I

was determined to make the most of our time together.

We ordered Polyburgers, with french fries and sodas. After the student waiter had taken our order, Jon sat back in his chair and looked at me.

"Well, you sure turned that chess game around, Kerry," he said, smiling.

"I did, didn't I?" I swept my hair back away from my forehead, hoping it didn't look too tangled after being under a hat and then a crown. "At least Bill wasn't mad at me. I don't think I could have stood it if he'd been really upset."

"Nah, Bill understands you." Jon was squinting in the dim light as if trying to see me better. "I wish *I* did."

That was a jolt. "What do you mean by that? There's nothing mysterious about me. What you see is all there is."

He laughed heartily at that. "I don't think so. I wish I could understand—well, what it is that makes you enjoy life so much. You just fling yourself into everything, no matter what the consequences. It's really pretty special, you know."

For once, I was at a loss for words. I felt a blush coming into my cheeks and a warm, satisfied glow inside my chest.

Jon went on to say, "I wish I could be that way—even just a little bit. But I guess us nerd types always worry about the consequences."

I gave him a severe look. "I told you to stop calling yourself a nerd! I won't tolerate it!"

Jon fell silent then, and toyed with the paper napkin by his place mat. I started feeling awkward, wondering what to say. The things that interested Jon—computers, the Math Club—were things I knew nothing about.

Ironically, that turned out to be a good place to start. I began asking him about the Math Club, and he talked freely and easily, with that sense of humor that always seemed to light up his face. I was interested in the things he liked, so it was perfectly easy to listen.

When our burgers arrived, we were discussing science-fiction films, and it wasn't any harder than talking to my own brother. By the time we'd finished our meal, we were gabbing about elementary school.

"I went to Waverly School up until fifth grade," I mentioned. "It was a good school. I had lots of friends, and I even got pretty good grades," I said with a laugh.

"I went to Greendale School," Jon said. "It was very hard for me. Kids made fun of me, lots of times, because I was always so serious about my studies and homework."

I felt a pang of sympathy for him. "But didn't it get easier when you went to Lincoln High?" I asked.

"Oh, sure. Even by middle school, I was put into high-level classes that were really challenging, with teachers who were glad to have an eager student." Jon laughed. "And I was lucky. I grew tall enough so that nobody dared make fun of me anymore."

It really made me sad to think of Jon being an unhappy little kid, and I said so.

"No, that's not true," he said, after giving it some thought. "Their teasing didn't really bother me. I was always happy, no matter what. I knew that what I was learning was more important than being pals with a lot of loudmouths. And besides, I had a few good friends who helped a lot."

Jon's words echoed in my head. *"A lot of loudmouths,"* I thought, feeling uneasy. I wondered if that was what *I* was. If so, had I always been that way? If I had gone to Jon's grade school, would I have been one of the kids who made fun of him? The idea that I might have been made me feel terrible.

"Let's talk about the chess game," Jon said suddenly, as though he wanted to change the topic. "What did you think of that snooty white queen? I'll bet you felt happy when she was captured and led away."

We laughed together. "I sure did. But the rest of the people were really nice, weren't they? It was a great experience, all around."

"It was. And you know what? You looked terrific in that queen's gown."

I was blushing again. I remembered how I'd flirted so shamelessly with him. "Well, you looked pretty good as a knight, too, Jon."

Then there was one of those moments of silence that usually fall in the middle of a great animated conversation. Neither of us could think of a thing to say to break the silence. It was lucky that our waiter came back with the check, or we might have sat there forever.

"Here you go," the waiter said cheerfully. "You people going to the concert out on the green this evening?"

"We didn't know there was one," Jon looked up at the waiter with interest. "What kind of concert?"

"It's a battle of the bands kind of thing. All sorts of music—rock, country, even some new wave, I suppose. And it's free."

"Oh, wouldn't that be fun?" I said quickly. I was beginning to like being on the college campus. Already I felt as though we were college students ourselves. I hated the thought of leaving, just when Jon and I were starting to communicate so well.

The waiter left, and Jon looked at me questioningly. "You're the queen, my lady, so it's up to you. Me, I'm just your humble knight."

I fell into the spirit of the thing. "In that case, Sir Jon, my faithful subject, my answer is yes. Let's go over to the concert!"

Chapter Ten

We strolled across the lawn because that's what we figured mature college students were supposed to do. We even laughed about it, and Jon said, "The slower we walk, the older we'll look, Kerry—I mean, Your Highness."

"Right," I agreed. "We might even look like grad students if we walk a little slower!"

"By the way, do you know where the green is?"

"No, I thought you did."

We laughed again. Jon asked a student for directions, and she told us we'd been going the wrong way. We had to go back, around the student union, and past the quad, which was four old brick dorms set in a square. After that, she'd said we should just follow our ears. We'd hear the bands getting warmed up on the green.

"What a great school," Jon said wistfully. "It *is* ugly in some ways as you said. But I love its oldness. And the way they've blended the newer buildings in with the older ones. Boy, I hope I get accepted here."

"Are you crazy? Of course you will," I assured him. I knew he'd gotten fantastic scores on the SATs.

It was a beautiful night, almost impossibly warm for October. "We've been lucky," I said in a dreamy voice. "A warm, sunny day for the chess game, and now a night that's almost perfect."

"Seems perfect to me," Jon agreed quietly in a hushed tone. I looked quickly up at his face, but his expression was unreadable, as it often was. I couldn't stand it.

"I wish I could understand *you*," I blurted out. "You make more mysterious remarks, Jon Madison, than anyone I've ever known. Or is it that I'm just too dumb to understand them?"

"You're not dumb, Kerry." He spoke firmly, in that deep, melodious voice of his. I felt shivers running along my spine. I wondered just what Jon was thinking.

Don't ask for miracles, Kerry, I told myself. *Just be glad you're with him, and don't try to figure out why he's here on a date with you. Or what he thinks of you.*

So I tried to relax. Jon and I reached the green and took a seat in the back, on a wooden bench under a tree. Chairs had been provided for the audience, but the bench seemed nicer.

Jon explained, "Her Highness the Queen shouldn't be sitting over there with all the rabble."

He really is playing up this queen business, I thought rather uncomfortably. I began to think again that Jon was just teasing me, playing a game because I had flirted during the chess game. That made it even more important for me to relax and not take anything seriously.

"I'm glad Bill took my camera bag with him," I said, settling on the bench and throwing my sweater over my shoulders. "I wouldn't want to get into any more trouble trying to photograph the musicians here."

"Oh, I don't know. It might have been fun." Jon was looking upward. "Let's see, you probably could hang by one foot from that fence over there—"

"Wise guy," I said, pretending to punch his arm. "You're as bad as Bill, the way you make fun of me."

"Oh? Does that mean I qualify as a second big brother?" he asked quietly. There was a hint of amusement in his voice, but at the same time, I sensed that he was asking me a very real question. And that maybe the answer I gave would be important.

I hesitated a moment. "I don't know if I need any more big brothers. Do you—do you think of me as a sister?"

His soft gray eyes were scanning my face, which must have been barely visible in the dim light that came from the concert stage. Jon looked as if he wanted to say something, but he just wasn't able to get the words out.

I helped him along. "Maybe you don't need any sisters, either. You haven't told me yet. Do you have any? Sisters or brothers, I mean?"

"Nope. I'm your classic lonely only child."

I didn't want to think of Jon being lonely. I wanted to give him a hug and be enfolded in his arms, right there under that tree on the Polytech campus. But of course I couldn't.

"How about cousins?" I asked quickly.

"I have a few cousins. Why?"

"Oh, because we have dozens. An enormous

family on both sides—the Fieldses and the Murphys."

"You're lucky," Jon said. "That must be fun on holidays."

"It is. Oh, look," I said, pointing. "The concert is about to start."

We settled back to listen to the music. Most of the rock songs were ones we knew. We even enjoyed the country tunes and found ourselves clapping our hands and stomping our feet along with the crowd.

Finally a band came on that played really slow, romantic songs. The music seemed to drift all around us, filling the soft, night air with a kind of magic. Both of us leaned back and relaxed, and suddenly, before I realized what was happening, Jon took my hand in his.

He didn't say a word. He just kept staring at the concert stage. But the silent message was there: "I like being with you, and you're not totally a sister to me, Kerry."

At least that was the way I read the message. So, wrapped in my romantic dreams, I put my head against Jon's shoulder for the rest of the concert. *We're really making progress,* I thought.

Maybe I hadn't been all-out crazy to fall in love with him. Maybe I had been right when I interpreted that smiling photo of Jon. Maybe he cared for me, even just a little.

"It's beginning to get a little chilly," Jon said after the romantic music had ended and the new-wave stuff began. "What do you think, Kerry? Should we try to catch a bus for home?"

I nodded, not wanting to break the magic of the moment, but realizing that he was right. It was late, and we had school the next day. It was time to go home.

On the bus we went back to talking and laughing and just plain having a good time. No holding hands or leaning on shoulders. It was a crowded public bus. We were "friends" again.

The bus let us off at the top of my street. We walked down the road with our arms almost brushing against each other, but not quite. Jon didn't take my hand again.

The row of maples along my street was lit by a sliver of a moon, and I thought how the shadows dancing across the road were somewhat like Jon and me. One minute something was there, the next minute it wasn't. The truth was, and I knew it all too well, Jon was shy and inexperienced when it came to girls.

So, when we reached the front pathway to

my house, I was trying to think of a way to show him that I cared.

"I had a wonderful time tonight, Jon," I said honestly.

"I did, too. It's an honor to be an escort to a queen."

"Stop teasing me. I'm serious."

"Oh, no you're not, Kerry. I don't think you know how to be serious."

We were almost to the doorstep, which was flooded with bright light from the outdoor lamp. I stopped short, right by the tall juniper bush, determined to avoid that light.

"Jon, please don't tell me that I'm never serious," I argued. "You don't know me at all, if you say a thing like that."

He stopped walking, too. "Probably I *don't* know you, Kerry. I told you I don't really understand what makes you tick."

I didn't know what to say. I didn't know how to tell him that he was someone really special to me. A girl can't just shoot off her mouth and say those words, can she?

But I did something just as impulsive. I snuggled up close to Jon and took his face in my hands. I still can't believe it to this day, but that's what I did. And I kissed him. Right on the lips. And even though I had shocked myself, the expression on Jon's face was even more amazing.

He returned my kiss, then pulled back just a tiny bit to stare at me. There was a look of total confusion on his face.

"I guess we both got carried away by that chess game, huh?" he said in a strained voice. "All that queen and knight business really put you in the mood for playing games, didn't it?"

"Playing games? No." I frowned. Maybe I'd been too impulsive in kissing him, but I wasn't playing any games.

"Cut it out, Kerry. I know you always date guys like Luke Russell, the Mr. Personality types."

I was crushed. "Maybe in the past I did, but only because—I don't know. I was always afraid of anyone smart like you."

"I'll tell you something, Kerry." Jon spoke sincerely and softly. "What *I'm* afraid of is playing games with you." His face was twisted with unhappiness.

"I'm not playing games, Jon, and I wish you'd stop saying that. I've loved being with you tonight. I've never had a better time—"

He leaned over to silence me with his mouth.

The kiss seemed to last forever, and yet it was only minutes, of course. I thought my heart was going to burst because I was so happy. Jon's mouth was warm and sweet. His kiss was not sloppy or clumsy. It was just right.

And yet I had the feeling that he was kissing me against his will. Against his better judgment.

Still, I threw my arms around his neck and moved closer to him, trying to show him that it was all right. It was OK for us to share a kiss, after the wonderful day and evening we'd had together.

We stayed in each other's arms for a while, a beautiful and magic moment, and then slowly we pulled apart. I watched Jon's face. He looked sad when he should have been happy.

"I've been wishing this would happen," I said breathlessly.

"Sure, Kerry," he said in a flat tone. "Just like all the other nutty stunts that you pull. See if you can capture the knight, just like in the chess game."

I felt as though cold water had been thrown at me, and I was standing there dripping wet—and afraid.

"No, Jon," I said carefully. "You've got that wrong. What I'm feeling now has nothing to do with the chess game."

"Aaah, Kerry." He leaned over and kissed my

cheek. "You're a cute little person, do you know that?"

It was a dismissal.

I knew his remark really meant, "You're a cute, dumb little person, and no one can ever take you seriously."

And I was terribly hurt.

"Naturally I'm not a math genius like Claudia," I said frostily. "But I'm not that dumb. I know when a boy is saying that he's not interested."

Now it was Jon's turn to look confused. "What does Claudia have to do with anything? I was just—"

"I guess you were just comparing me with her," I finished for him. I squared my shoulders and tried to stand as tall as I could. "Don't bother. I suppose you're right. Just chalk up one more crazy stunt in the life of Kerry Fields."

"Kerry—"

"Don't." I put up my hand and touched his lips. The contact with him made my fingers tingle, but I wouldn't let him know it. Was it possible that just minutes ago those lips had been pressed against mine?

"Don't say any more," I finished. "I had a wonderful time tonight, and I thank you. Good night, Jon."

He didn't seem to be moving away, so I made the first move. I started toward my front door. I could be stubborn when the need arose.

"Oh. Will you be needing a ride home?" I thought to ask, just as I reached the steps. "Either Bill or I could drive you."

"No." His voice was flat, stripped of all emotion. "No, thanks. I'll walk home."

And he disappeared quietly into the night.

"I hate brainy boys! I absolutely hate them!" I threw those statements toward Bill, who was sitting at the kitchen table buried in a mound of thick, incomprehensible engineering books.

"Oh, is that so?" Bill didn't even look up.

Well, he certainly seemed unconcerned about my problems. I pushed things about in the refrigerator, deciding at last on a glass of milk to cool down my anger.

I gave Bill a scathing look because he was too wrapped up in his studies to talk to me.

"I seriously doubt that you really hate Jon Madison," Bill finally observed with a lazy, know-it-all drawl.

"Well, that just shows what you know. Nothing. Nothing at all about a girl's heart."

"Has your heart been broken, Kerry?" Bill was still in a teasing mood. Couldn't he see that I was in no frame of mind to be laughed at?

I didn't answer him. Instead I stuffed my face with one of Mom's extra-fudgy brownies, and washed it down with more milk.

"Kerry. You didn't look as though you hated Jon all afternoon, out there on the chess-board."

"Don't you remind me of that chess game, too! I made a fool of myself, I'm sure." I spat out the words. "Well, I won't do it again. I am simply through with the high-IQ set."

Bill's voice became more serious. "Do you want to talk about it, Ker?"

But it was too late. I was no longer about to share my feelings with that insensitive brother of mine.

"Afraid not." I poured another glass of milk. "And another thing. Your Polytech campus is really dumb."

"*What?*"

"That's right. They probably don't even teach photography in that stupid school. And nothing at all about life. Bunch of nerds run-ning around with calculators and slide rules on their belts—"

"Now wait just one minute, there—"

"And worst of all," I finished up dramatically, "the Polyburgers are gross. Just as gross as their french fries."

"Kerry!"

"Good night, Bill."

I made a sweeping exit from the kitchen. I wanted to find my puppy and cuddle up with her in my room. I had a feeling I was headed for a good, long cry, and I needed a sympathetic friend.

Chapter Eleven

"You've got some really excellent photos here, Kerry," Mr. Shannon told me on Monday morning. I was showing him a folder of my human chess game pictures.

Instead of spending Sunday night crying over Jon, I had stayed up late developing the photographs at home. And I was really pleased with the way they had turned out. At least I got results in some areas, anyway.

"So which one do you think I should enter in the contest?" I asked, trying to peer over Mr. Shannon's shoulder.

"This one—the sweeping scene of the entire

chessboard. And also this one, although it obviously wasn't taken at the chess game."

"What?" I looked and saw the picture he meant. It was the one of Jon I'd taken in the computer room that morning long ago—the first, unsmiling, picture of Jon bent over the computer printout. I hadn't even meant for that to be in the folder!

"This is a very good photo, Kerry." Mr. Shannon held it away from him to get a better look at it. "The composition, the lighting, and, quite honestly, the subject." He turned to give me a shrewd glance. "A person might almost think that the photographer was, um, extremely fond of her subject."

A week earlier I would have blushed, giving away the fact that I was crazy about Jon. But everything had changed since then.

"He was a subject, that's all, Mr. Shannon," I said in a cold, clipped voice. "Just a random senior who I happened to spot near the computers."

"Mmm-hmm." Mr. Shannon winked at me. "And how does it happen that this same random subject manages to appear in the other pictures, too—as a dashing young knight on the college chessboard?"

"Gosh. Must be pure coincidence." I felt no

guilt at all about stretching the truth. A girl has to protect herself in sticky situations.

"Yes, I see. Pure coincidence. Well, at any rate, in my opinion you have two excellent entries right here for the photo contest."

"I never thought of sending the computer room photo."

"You really ought to. I think it's a gem."

Just then the door of the darkroom opened, and Peter Ascari, one of Mr. Shannon's prize photography students, peered out.

"I'm all done here," he announced. "The darkroom is available for anyone else."

Peter came out to show off his latest photographs, which were outdoor scenes, his specialty. There were shots of trees, wild animals, and all sorts of moss formations on rocks. They were pretty good.

In fact, *Peter* looked pretty good all of **a** sudden.

I had decided that I had to forget about Jon, and I'd been searching for a way to do it. After Jon had dismissed me the night before I had found myself wishing that I could meet another boy, who would make me forget him. I didn't want it to be Luke Russell; that was an impossible situation. But Peter—maybe Peter was the "artistic someone" that I'd told my brother I'd meet someday.

Peter even *looked* artistic. He was short, in fact not much more than an inch or two taller than I. He had a few freckles around his nose, and a thatch of straight hair that always seemed to be uncombed. Yes, he was definitely the offbeat artistic type, just right for me.

I waited until Mr. Shannon went over to talk with another student, who came in with a calculus problem.

"Say, Peter? Your pictures are really good, you know that?"

"Yes, I do know." His big blue eyes were half-joking and half-serious. One thing Peter had was a large ego; I knew that from our advanced photography class. But I suspected he also had a sense of humor.

"I've been thinking," I said. "Remember when Mr. Shannon talked about wilderness safaris? Going out to get pictures of wildlife?"

"Of course I remember it, Kerry. I've already done it. How do you suppose I accumulated this marvelous nature portfolio?"

I couldn't tell whether he was kidding or not. I didn't care. I was determined to get a date with him, one way or another.

"Could we—" I hesitated long enough to appear helpless and shy. "Do you think you might take me on one of those safaris sometime? I'd love to learn from an expert like you."

He fell for it. His chest expanded visibly, and he tried to stand a little taller. "I don't see why not, Kerry. I'm sure you can learn from my photographic methods."

"Oh, yes," I agreed.

Is this really me? I thought, *groveling for a stupid date with a boy, just because he might be the artistic type? Oh, Kerry, you fool.*

But I stuck to my plan. Peter and I finally settled on a date the next Sunday morning.

"It's important to get out there at the crack of dawn," he told me seriously. "This is exactly like hunting. Your subjects, the wildlife, are only out really early. And as they say, the early bird catches the worm, Kerry." He chuckled at his own joke. I didn't.

Maybe it was a bad idea, after all, I thought as I left Mr. Shannon's classroom. But, on the other hand, the worst thing that could happen would be that I'd learn more about taking wildlife photos. Where was the harm in that?

I was sure that it was going to be a miserable week for me. I knew I still had to face Jon because of his and Bill's chess moves. I also knew that I loved him more than ever, especially after our date and the two kisses we had shared afterward.

But I knew, too, that he had brushed me off quite firmly, and so I had to face facts. Jon was never going to care for me. He was Polytech material, and I might just as well enroll in clown school.

Still haunted by thoughts of Sunday night, I trudged along the school hallway. The way Jon had kissed me, so tenderly and yet so firmly, was enough to make me go crazy. Why had he done it? Everything about that boy was such a mystery to me.

Just then Cindy caught up with me. "Hi, stranger. It seems as though I never see you anymore. How was that chess thing over the weekend?"

"Don't ask," I groaned.

"Oh, boring, huh? I thought so. Chess always did seem like a dull game to me."

I stared at Cindy. I'd found out that chess was far from dull. In fact, what was it Jon had said? *"In chess, there are always at least two things happening at once."* That had seemed like an important, cryptic statement at the time. But still, try as I might, I couldn't figure out what he'd meant by it.

"So how are things with you and Phil?" I asked politely. I knew Cindy was dying to tell me.

And she did. She didn't stop talking until

we got to our next class, biology. She and Phil were doing just fine, as it turned out. I was glad for her.

But, needless to say, I was sad for *me*.

"Oh, by the way, I have a date with someone new," I mentioned just as we reached the classroom door. "Peter Ascari. He's taking me on a wilderness trek next Sunday. For nature photos. Before the birds even wake up."

"Oh, Kerry, you are a masochist," Cindy said, shivering. "Why do you get yourself involved in those kinds of dates, anyway?"

I smiled thinly. "At least this is better than going out with Luke Russell, isn't it? Peter is a talented photographer, and we'll have a lot in common."

Cindy gave me a knowledgeable look. "I had the impression that you liked Jon Madison."

"Did you?"

"Come on, you know it was true. You can't fool old Cindy." She was right. I had known Cindy for too long.

"Maybe we can talk about it another time," I whispered. "Maybe you can—maybe you can help, Cin. Maybe you can teach me some way to forget about Jon."

I suppose I sounded pathetic, for Cindy put a hand on my shoulder. And to my horror, I felt as if I was about to start crying! I couldn't do that, not right outside the classroom with everybody milling all around us.

"Wait a minute! Maybe this will make you feel better," Cindy said, suddenly remembering something. "I have a note for you. Jon gave it to me before lunch."

"A note? For me?" I took it eagerly and unfolded the piece of paper.

"Bishop to D7" was all it said, in Jon's strong, firm handwriting. My heart went plummeting to the floor.

Cindy made a sound of disgust. "Oh, it's just his stupid old chess move, isn't it? I'm sorry, Kerry."

I began to wonder if Jon had given the chess move to Cindy because he didn't even want to see me anymore. Was he so annoyed with me that he planned to give the chess moves to Cindy from now on?

I stood there staring at the small piece of paper, and I realized something. There was one thing I never should have said to Jon when I'd kissed him: "Chalk up one more crazy stunt in the life of Kerry Fields."

Then, stupidly, I *did* start to cry.

I have never had any patience with girls who cry in public. It's certainly not my style. But suddenly I found myself doing it, and it seemed as though the entire student body of

Lincoln High School went passing by at that moment, staring at me with curiosity.

The gossip spreaders would have a great day. Kerry Fields, crying? Unheard of. I was known as a tough little cookie who could do anything and would put up with no nonsense. Of all people, no one would ever expect to catch Kerry the Flash weeping in a school hallway!

"What's going on out here?" our biology teacher asked in a concerned tone as she came to the door and shooed away some of the kids who were crowding around.

"I think Kerry might have a headache, Ms. Payne," Cindy said.

"Why don't you go down to the nurse, Kerry? I imagine she'll be able to give you some aspirin."

"Thanks, Ms. Payne," I said. She turned back into the classroom, and I turned to Cindy. "Thanks. I'll do something nice for you, someday," I promised in a low voice.

"Just don't ever teach me to play chess," Cindy quipped. "It sounds like the road to Heartbreak Hill is paved with chess games, if you ask me."

I told the nurse the truth. I didn't need an aspirin, I needed a little understanding because I was in love with someone who didn't love me.

Mrs. Taylor clucked with sympathy. "I know just how you feel, dear." She actually put a tea-kettle on to boil. "Don't think you're the first student to come in here with a problem like that."

"So what do you tell them? What will help?" I asked curiously. I had always thought Mrs. Taylor was a pretty special person, for a school nurse.

Her face clouded over. "I'm afraid I don't have any easy answers, Kerry. Only time will heal your heartbreak, but I promise you it will feel just a little better every day. In a month or two you'll look back on today and laugh at it."

"I don't know about that," I said, settling back on her couch. "I realized just now that I said something to this certain boy that—"

Just then there was a knock, and Jon poked his head in through the health-office door.

"Excuse me. Kerry? Someone told me you were, er, sick, just a little while ago."

I couldn't believe it. Jon had cared enough about me to leave whatever classroom he was in, to find out if I was all right.

"I was in study hall, and someone said you were crying outside the bio lab," he explained. He looked worried. "I thought—that is, I know

120

it's none of my business, but I wondered—if you're sick, would it help if I drove you home? I have my mother's car today."

Mrs. Taylor was watching us with an amused look on her face. I think she was making an educated guess as to who the boy was that I was in love with. "If you two will excuse me," she said, heading toward the door. "I have to take this report to the principal's office."

Jon came in, concern showing in his light gray eyes. *He looks wonderful,* I thought. He was wearing a blue shirt that made his eyes look almost blue, and a really nice blazer. He was so dressed up that I felt like asking him what the occasion was.

But, of course, I didn't.

"I'm going to tell you the truth about why I was crying, Jon," I said. "It was because I opened that note from you that Cindy gave me. Your chess move."

He looked startled. "You cried because of my chess move?"

"No. I started crying because—well, because I knew that I had said some crummy things to you last night, and I wanted to tell you that I didn't mean them."

Jon stared at me but didn't say a word.

121

"It's the truth, Jon. When Cindy gave me the chess move, I figured you probably never wanted to see me again—"

He stuffed his hands into his pockets. "No. That wasn't it. I just happened to see Cindy before I saw you. And I still don't see why you were crying."

"You don't know much about girls, do you?" I said, and sighed. "I felt bad because I'd said 'Chalk up another stunt for Kerry Fields,' or whatever it was. Remember?"

"Yes." His face was absolutely still.

"I didn't *mean* that, Jon. And it bothered me. So now I've explained myself. I feel better."

"Kerry, you're really confusing me."

"Don't I always? Hey, as long as you're here, I just remembered something." I pulled my portfolio of pictures out of the stack of books I'd been carrying. "Do you mind if I send this photo to a contest? It's a picture of you, Jon, and Mr. Shannon says it's a real winner."

He looked at it without much interest.

"Oh, yeah, my Nerd-of-the-Year picture."

"Stop saying that. So is it all right with you if I submit it? I want to send in that one and—this one." I showed him my shot of the human chess game.

He whistled in appreciation. "Now *that* is a good photograph, Kerry. I'm really impressed."

"Thank you," I said. I felt good. I knew it was a really professional photograph. And I certainly had risked my neck, going up the tree, to get it!

Jon still looked concerned about something. "Kerry, about the reason you were crying."

"Don't worry about it." I smiled brightly to show him that it didn't matter anymore. "I've learned my lesson. I'll never cry in the halls of school again. Word gets around too fast in this school, don't you think?"

"That's not what I—"

But he stopped in midsentence, and I couldn't tell what he had planned to say. He was staring at me helplessly, and I thought again about those kisses we had shared on my front lawn. I knew there would never be another chance.

"Look, I hope there are no hard feelings, Jon. I really had a wonderful time with you last night."

"I did, too."

"So there you are. And now I wish you all the happiness in the world with Claudia Martin. Really, I do. In fact, I have a pretty special date myself. I'm going out with Peter Ascari, the mad photographer. You know him, don't you? I think we're going to make a great team."

He looked startled. "Oh. Yes, you two would probably make a very good—team."

"That's right. People should stick to their own kind, don't you think? That's why you and Claudia will do quite well together. You have math and computers and all that in common."

"Kerry—"

I stood up. "So it's all settled? I can send in this photo of you to the contest?"

"Yes, sure, if Mr. Shannon told you to. But I don't—" He didn't finish whatever he was going to say.

Then Mrs. Taylor came back into the room.

"Everything's fine now, Mrs. Taylor," I said brightly. "I feel great. Thanks for everything; I won't even need the cup of tea."

"I'm glad, dear." She shut off the boiling tea-kettle. She was looking from Jon to me with a puzzled expression.

"I'd better get back to my biology class," I told them both. "Thanks, Jon, for coming down here. You really did help."

I took off before he could say another word.

Chapter Twelve

I walked back to biology thinking it wasn't going to be the most miserable of weeks, after all. At least Jon and I were friends again. And I didn't have to avoid looking at him or feel that he hated me because I'd been such a creep the night before.

Things went on much as they had been before the human chess game. I continued to bring in Bill's chess moves, and Jon still gave me the small slips of paper for Bill. Whenever we met, I smiled politely and Jon smiled politely, and that was that.

Jon didn't make any attempt, after our talk in the health office, to speak to me other than about the chess moves. It was as though that Sunday night had never happened.

Except that in my heart, there was a big, aching hole that I couldn't seem to get rid of, no matter what I tried. And I tried everything—plenty of photography, lots of work at the animal hospital, even some jogging. And I hate jogging with a passion.

Nothing helped me stop thinking of those minutes I'd spent in Jon Madison's arms.

It was so unfair! I loved Jon so much, and I had to make myself forget about him. I had to. Brainy boys and idiotic girls did not belong together.

So I tried to look forward to my date with Peter Ascari. Maybe going out with Peter would be the thing to help me forget my knight.

Sunday morning finally arrived. We started out, as Peter had warned me, at the crack of dawn. I didn't even have time for breakfast. And it was so dark and cold. My eyes were bleary from too little sleep, and my body was crying out for something to eat. My system doesn't begin to work until I've had some juice and my apple-raisin cereal.

"Sorry, but we have to get out there ahead of the deer," Peter insisted. We drove quickly in his father's car to a wilderness trail called Steep Rock Hill. It was appropriately named.

"We're climbing up a cliff," I said, huffing and puffing but trying not to sound like a complainer. "I mean, we are talking sheer, upward cliff here, Peter."

"Of course. We can't take the roundabout path because the deer nearby might smell us. We could scare them away. You don't want that to happen, do you?"

"Oh, no. Of course not." I was gasping for air.

"You know, I always like to go out photographing in extreme weather." Peter seemed very proud of that fact. "I mean, a blizzard would be ideal. Any sort of precipitation is excellent."

"Are you nuts? Your camera equipment would get all wet."

"*Aha!* Exactly what every photographer thinks! Therefore, no one else is out there taking the photos that I am getting! And I protect my equipment with small tarps and plain old plastic bags. You see?"

"I see. Peter Ascari gets the blizzard photos and becomes world famous." I stopped for a second to catch my breath. "Gee, wouldn't a typhoon be lovely? Or even a full-scale earthquake—maybe one that registers a seven on the Richter scale?"

He nodded in agreement. "*Extremes*, that's what I look for." He swung his agile body up and over, onto the flat peak at the top of the cliff. I tried to do the same; I wasn't going to show any signs of weakening.

We spent the next two hours huddled in the cold morning air, waiting for the deer to show up at the spring below. A few other wild animals—a wild turkey, a raccoon, and a baby rabbit—wandered by, and we photographed them. But the deer didn't seem to be around.

"They sense we're here," Peter whispered. "Deer are acutely sensitive to people." He glared at me. "Maybe it would be better if I came alone, from now on. No doubt they hear you talking, Kerry, and stay away."

By that time, I didn't care if we ever saw deer. In fact, I no longer cared about my original mission, either, which had been to try to land Peter Ascari as my "artistic" boyfriend.

"I'm hungry and cold," I grumbled.

"You're a pest, Kerry," he grumbled right back.

I didn't understand, I thought. Peter was supposed to be the right kind of boy for me. The chemistry should have been right! He and I had so much in common, and we were both fanatics about photography. So why did the whole thing feel so terribly wrong?

I looked over at Peter, crouched down ready with his camera, and decided he took himself much too seriously. Now Jon, who really *was* a genius and had reason to be proud of himself, was never like that.

I'd never thought about it before, but there it was. Jon never bragged and never showed off his superior intelligence. Neither did Bill, for that matter.

In fact, Jon had never treated me as if I were stupid. It was only my own inferiority complex that had made me feel that way.

"I think I'd like to go home, Peter," I finally said.

"I do, too. This just hasn't worked out too well, Kerry. I might as well be honest with you. I think it's a hindrance to have a partner."

"I'm sure it is," I said, wondering how I'd ever considered a romance with that obnoxious boy. I was also thinking about pancakes, coffee, and maybe a plateful of my mother's blueberry muffins.

We took the roundabout trail going back, and Peter managed to look sulky the whole time. I couldn't believe that a boy of his age could be so childish.

On the way home, he asked casually, "Did you send your entry into that contest?"

"Oh, sure. Did you enter, too?"

"Of course I did." He sounded really impatient. "I have to admit, I thought your photo of that chess game thing was a most unusual shot."

"Thanks, Peter." But I looked at him closely and realized that he was not really complimenting me. He was jealous. I was almost certain of it. He was jealous because he was afraid that I might have a better photograph than any of his for the statewide contest.

"Good luck with your entry," I said cheerfully. He didn't wish the same for me, I noticed. "And listen, thanks for taking me out this morning, even if it didn't work out the way you wanted."

"You're welcome," Peter said. What a grump he was! I had never been so glad to get back home in my whole life.

I really hate the word *depressed*, but that's how I felt after my disastrous date with Peter Ascari. Besides being embarrassed about the whole thing, I had started to wonder if *any* boy could love me.

After an enormous breakfast, I curled up in my room to listen to some music and just think, which is what I do whenever I'm feeling down. Pillbox accompanied me, charging into my room dragging a huge rawhide bone with her. We played tug-of-war with the bone for a while, but even Pillbox couldn't distract me from my problems.

This is ridiculous, I thought. Just because Jon Madison didn't love me back didn't mean I had to mope around forever. There were plenty of things in life besides a very intelligent boy with beautiful gray eyes. I resolved to forget about Jon and get on with my life.

But of course that was easier said than done. Jon and I still had to see each other because of the chess game. I was beginning to wish that the stupid game would end, one of these weeks. It was very difficult for me to be so polite and friendly to Jon when, inside, my heart was breaking into millions of pieces.

Especially hard were the times when I saw him with Claudia. She seemed to be chasing him all over school, asking questions about the Math Club or jabbering about her new computer gizmos. Truthfully, he didn't look all that interested in her, but that was probably because his mind was always in the clouds to begin with.

One Saturday, a few weeks after my date with Peter, I ran into Jon and his mother at

Blanton's Department Store on my way home from working at the animal hospital. Dr. Turner had needed some extra help, so I told him I would work for a couple of Saturdays.

Of course I looked my absolute worst. My hair was uncombed, and I felt dirty after cleaning animal cages all day.

I had run into Blanton's to buy film so I could take a few candid shots at the senior car wash the next day.

"Kerry. Hi," Jon said, a big grin transforming his face as soon as he spotted me. "Mom, this is Kerry Fields, a friend from school."

"I've heard quite a bit about you, Kerry," said Mrs. Madison with a smile. She was slim and elegant, with brown hair that was pulled back in a neat bun. Her cream-colored suit looked expensive and was coordinated perfectly with a brown silk blouse and matching brown shoes and purse. She was obviously a career woman of some sort.

Next to her, I felt like a sloppy little farmhand.

"Kerry's brother is the guy I've been playing chess with," Jon explained further.

"Oh, yes," she answered. "And you two were in the human chess game together, if I remember correctly."

We both nodded, but neither of us spoke. I didn't trust myself to say something that wouldn't betray my feelings for Jon, that wouldn't make it perfectly obvious how important that date had been to me.

I didn't know why Jon didn't say anything, but I didn't think I'd like his reason, whatever it was.

"It's so nice to meet you, Kerry," Mrs. Madison said. "Jon says that you're a very talented photographer."

"Oh. Thank you," I said simply. I was surprised that Jon had mentioned me at all to his mother.

"I have to go upstairs to children's wear," she said, still smiling at me. "I have to buy a baby-shower gift for a woman at work. Goodbye now, Kerry. I'm glad I met you."

"Uh—nice to meet you, too," I said. I was a little surprised when Jon said, "Mom, I'll meet you back here in half an hour, all right?"

Jon and I were left standing there by the camera department.

"Can I ask you a favor, Kerry? Do you mind?"

"No, of course not."

He whispered as though he didn't want anyone else to hear. "Well, it's my mother's birthday in a few days, and I want to get her a really

133

special gift. But I'm having trouble. Would you help me pick something out?"

"Sure."

"I usually get her the same old perfume, her favorite brand. But this year she's turning forty, and I wanted to get something special. I was thinking of earrings."

He was so cute! I wanted to put my hand on his shoulder and tell him everything was OK. He seemed so lost when it came to shopping for women.

"Earrings are rough," I said. "Every woman has such individual taste, you know. A pair that I might pick out would probably be all wrong for your mom." I thought back to the elegant woman I'd just met. "But I'll tell you what. Silk scarves are very popular this year, and I'll bet we could find one she'd like."

"A scarf? I don't know—"

"Sure. She'll love one. She's a very classy, stylish lady. And if the color isn't right, she can always exchange it for another one."

Jon looked at me with relief.

"I really appreciate this, Kerry. I'm always at a loss when it comes to shopping."

I laughed. "So is Bill. I'm used to helping boys shop. Come on, we'll find something really elegant for your mother."

We did, after more than twenty minutes and

after examining every silk scarf in Blanton's. That it took so long to make a choice was my fault. I did everything to put off making a final choice because I was so happy to be with Jon again. I told myself that I was playacting again, just like back on the chessboard with me as the queen and Jon as the knight. But we felt so right together, even though I knew Jon didn't think we were.

I asked the saleswoman to box and gift wrap the scarf.

"I didn't even know they'd do that," Jon admitted. "I certainly am glad I ran into you, Kerry."

"I'm glad you did, too," I said, without thinking. I felt myself getting all red-faced. I hated that. I'd never been prone to blushing before. But I *loved* being there with Jon, and I felt good that I had been able to do something to help him.

I love you so much, Jon, I thought sadly. I wished I could have been more like Claudia and less like myself. If I had been, maybe he would love me, too.

Jon seemed reluctant to leave. But he had to meet his mother in just a few minutes, so there was no way to tell if he would have stayed with me longer.

His mother, I thought, was a lot like

Claudia, even though she was warm and friendly. Jon had grown up with a lady who was cool and sensible. She was probably as brilliant as he was; maybe she was even a vice-president of some giant corporation.

He certainly didn't need gooney little Kerry.

"Well, I hope your mother likes the birthday gift," I said. To my embarrassment, I was fighting back the tears that threatened to spill down my cheeks because I hated to leave him. "Tell her that forty's not so bad. My father reached it this year, and he didn't seem to mind."

Jon smiled. "Yes, but maybe it's different for a woman."

"Maybe."

My eyes were locked into his. Those expressive, gray eyes sparkled under the bright lights of Blanton's, shining brighter than any diamonds. *I wouldn't mind turning forty,* I thought, *if I could always gaze into those eyes!*

"Kerry—"

"Yes?"

He didn't go on. He was silent for a long, drawn-out minute. Then he took my hand awkwardly, and shook it.

"I really want to thank you. For helping me with the gift."

A handshake. All I could think of was the melting kiss he had surprised me with that wonderful night, and he gave me a handshake.

"You're welcome," I said much too formally.

"I suppose you and Peter are quite a team these days. Taking photographs, I mean."

"Not exactly." I stuffed my hands into my pockets. "I don't suppose you've heard from any of those colleges you applied to for early decision yet?"

"No. Not yet." He turned when the saleswoman handed him the gift-wrapped package. "That really is pretty," he told her. He still seemed amazed that anyone would gift wrap a package for him.

"I have to get home now," I said reluctantly. We were still looking at each other in a sad, haunting way. "I was helping Dr. Turner at the animal hospital today, and I really need a bath."

"Sure." He cast his eyes down. "Say hello to Bill for me, will you?"

"Sure."

Finally I turned and left the store. I didn't even remember to buy the film I needed.

Chapter Thirteen

One afternoon a short time later, I broke down and told Bill how I felt about Jon. This time he wasn't busy studying, and he listened.

"I can't get that boy out of my mind," I confessed. We were sitting out in our backyard, staring at the autumn leaves as they tumbled to the ground. Bill was resting up after a marathon of hard exams, and I was just in the mood for some fresh air.

"Jon's a nice guy." Bill stretched out his long legs across the picnic bench. "Why do you make such a problem out of it, Kerry?"

"Because he doesn't want me, that's why." I

squinted my eyes into the sun and followed a golden leaf that was falling.

"I don't know about that, Kerry. From what you've told me, you two hit it off really well on that date. First the chess game, then dinner and the concert—"

"And then the brush-off. Really, Bill. He kissed me on the cheek and said I was a cute little person, or something equally demeaning."

Bill didn't laugh. He seemed to be thinking.

"Maybe he didn't intend it to be demeaning. Maybe he was just—backing off. He probably just needed time to think about what was happening."

I kicked at a clump of leaves. "You guys and your thinking. That's your whole trouble. You think so much that you can't see what's really going on."

Bill sat up. "That's probably it, kiddo. Jon probably doesn't see what's going on—I mean, that you care for him."

"Of course not. That's obvious. He thinks I just want to play games. He thinks I got carried away by that queen and knight business."

I stood up and walked over to a sagging, bare-branched forsythia bush. It looked as pitiful as I felt.

"Oh, Bill, if only I could be smarter! Why

couldn't I have been born with the brains, instead of you?"

"Now you're being ridiculous," Bill scolded. "There's absolutely nothing wrong with your brains, Kerry Ann Fields. You're just as smart as anyone I know."

"Oh, sure."

"You just were never the scholarly type, that's all. That doesn't mean you're not smart. You've always wanted a varied social life, and action, and lots of unconventional things to do. Maybe you became the way you are because people were always comparing the two of us and calling you the cute one."

"You mean maybe I was programmed to be the way I am?"

He held up his hands helplessly. "I don't know, honestly. I do know that you could be on the high honor roll, if you wanted to be. But somewhere along the line, you chose to be—Kerry."

"Kerry the Flash."

"Whatever. The thing is, there's nothing wrong with the person you are, Kerry. Nothing!"

"Yeah? Then how come Jon isn't after me with telephone calls and offers of dates? Because he prefers intelligent girls like Claudia, that's why."

"And you want to make yourself over, into a Claudia?"

"I wish I could. If it would make Jon notice me, I would."

"Oh, Kerry. I hope you don't try to do that. All a person can be is what they are. Even Shakespeare said it: 'This above all, to thine own self be true—' "

"Oh, sure. Go ahead. Quote Shakespeare at me at a time like this. Make me feel even stupider than ever!"

"The time is always right for Shakespeare, and I think I've had about enough of your self-pity."

He stalked over to the outdoor faucet, gave it a turn, and picked up the end of the green garden hose. He pointed the nozzle right at me.

"Don't you dare!" I shrieked. I was afraid he'd really do it. Bill could be crazy when it came to things like that. "I'd catch pneumonia at this time of year, Bill—"

He came closer, an evil look in his eye.

"You're going to get it, lady."

"Bill, don't be stupid. I do not deserve this."

"Oh, yes you do. Unless you repeat after me. 'I am Kerry Fields, and I am a person of worth.' "

"That's silly. I will not—"

"You will, or you'll be showered with water."
He aimed the hose nozzle right at my face.

"All right, all right." I took a deep breath. "I am Kerry Fields, and I am a person . . . of worth."

"Say it with conviction," Bill threatened.

I stuck my chin way out and spoke loudly and clearly. "I am a person of *worth*!"

Bill grinned. "That's better."

He squeezed the nozzle, anyway. No water came out.

"I knew Dad had already turned off the outside water for the winter," he told me. "But at least I made you stop whining."

I didn't really believe I was a worthy person, though. Not until November 15, that is, when there was a surprise announcement on the loudspeaker.

It happened during English class, oddly enough, the only class that I had with Jon.

"Your attention, please," said Mr. Farber, our principal. Then there was a high-pitched wail, as was usual with our school's PA system.

"May I have your attention, please," Mr. Farber repeated. "We have several important items of news."

Every student shifted restlessly in his seat.

Announcements were always incredibly boring.

"A very exciting thing has occurred," Mr. Farber said. "We have just received notification from the State High-School Photography Contest that Lincoln High School has a first-place winner."

Suddenly I was finding it hard to breathe. Could it be that one of my pictures had won? Or was it something that Peter Ascari had submitted?

Mr. Farber ended the suspense. "Our winner is none other than Miss Kerry Fields, the girl who's been nicknamed Kerry the Flash during her years at Lincoln High."

I felt the bottom drop out of my stomach. Had I really heard him right? Had he said I was the first-place winner?

"Kerry is the winner of the highest award in the entire contest, Best Overall Photograph," Mr. Farber went on, as if he had heard me. "She won with a photo entitled 'A Bird's-eye View of Human Chess Pieces.' Congratulations, Kerry."

He was silenced by another electronic shriek, and then our English class began to cheer!

"Congratulations, Kerry!" "Good work,

Kerry." "That's wonderful, Kerry. I'll bet this will get you a scholarship to art college."

They all talked and congratulated me at once, and Mr. Bandero didn't even try to restore order in the classroom. He looked as pleased as everyone else. He kept reminding the class of the time I'd popped out from under his desk, and wanted to know why that shot of *him* hadn't been the winning one.

Jon sat at his desk smiling, saying nothing. He looked really glad for me, but he didn't try to get through the crowd of well-wishers congregating around my desk.

I am a person of worth, I thought with dizziness. *Bill was right. I really do have a talent, and I'm learning how to use it. This has to be the greatest moment of my whole life!*

Then Mr. Farber's voice interrupted again.

"Now I have an announcement of a different sort," he said. "Three seniors at Lincoln High have just been named finalists in the National Merit Scholarship Program. As you know, this means that these students' SAT scores rank among the top in the nation.

"The three students are Claudia Martin, Jon Madison, and Robert Chang. Let's hear congratulations for these students of distinction!"

At that, it seemed that the whole school

rang out with cheers. I was glad for Jon, truly glad, but at the same time, I felt as if I were a giant balloon that was slowly deflating.

Quickly I turned to Jon and said, "Congratulations. That's the greatest honor any high-school student can win."

The bell finally rang, and I tried to pull all my notebooks together so I could make a fast exit. I wanted to get away from Jon.

Instead, I dropped everything, and all my belongings scattered across the floor.

"I'll help her pick them up," Jon said to everyone who offered to help. He actually shooed the whole class away.

Then quietly and efficiently he helped me to gather my papers, books, pencils, and pens. I didn't say a word. The classroom emptied out completely; even Mr. Bandero left.

Finally everything was picked up, and Jon looked at me with a warm, happy smile. It was almost the same smile I'd captured in the photograph weeks before. Almost, but not quite.

"I want to congratulate you, Kerry," he said with sincerity. "I was so happy to hear your good news. I know how much the contest meant to you."

The genuine warmth in his voice made me snap. I don't know why, but the tension that had been building up inside of me just broke loose.

"You want to congratulate *me*?" I blurted out. "Oh, come on, Jon. That was just another one of Kerry's crazy pranks."

"No, Kerry. I don't think so at all. I think—"

"I don't care what you think," I said coldly. "I wouldn't be able to understand your thought processes, anyway, we all know that."

"Kerry, what's wrong with you? I only wanted to give you my congratulations—"

"Don't bother. You three are the people to be congratulated. National Merit Scholarship finalists—that's incredible. And it's only the beginning of exciting things for you, Jon. So please don't waste your time talking to 'cute' little me."

"Kerry—"

My heart almost broke at that moment. Jon looked so confused and tormented that I almost wanted to apologize. But once my temper flared, there was no turning back.

"Forget it, Jon. I've been unusually stupid, that's all." I stopped to wipe away a tear that was threatening to drop from my eye. "I saw that picture I took of you, and I thought the smile was just for me, but I was wrong! But still, when we had such a good time at the concert, I thought again—but that's where my stupidity came in."

"Kerry, what are you talking about?"

My chin went up. "I'm talking about kisses that you didn't mean and games that *you* shouldn't have tried to play. Hey, just leave me alone, Jon. I'm not thinking straight at all."

"You certainly aren't," he said quietly. "Look, Kerry, I think we need to have a talk."

"I think we *don't*." I raced away from him. He caught up with me easily because his legs were so much longer, but I managed to push my way into the hallway traffic.

"Kerry, will you wait a minute?" I heard him calling, but I just kept moving. Stupid, stupid me. I had let him know how much I cared. It was bad enough that I'd kissed him on the night of the chess game. Now I had spilled all my secret thoughts!

Chapter Fourteen

Kerry "the pawn" was on strike from then on. I simply told Bill that I refused to be the go-between any longer. If he wanted to continue his chess game, he'd have to make his own arrangements to get the moves to Jon.

"You're crazy, Kerry," Bill said, shaking his head.

"Yes, I am. I'm crazy enough to know that I don't want to get my hopes up for that boy anymore. And that means that I don't want to see him all the time with your chess moves!"

"Kerry, you won the highest photography award in the state! Doesn't that tell you something about your worth? Or do I have to squirt you with the garden hose for real this time?"

"Give it up, Bill," I snapped. I was washing the dishes and beginning to fear that he might reach around me and spray me with the spray hose by the sink.

Bill glared at me. "Did you inform Jon of this strike of yours, too?"

"Yes, I did. I told him through Cindy that I was no longer willing to be the pawn."

"And what did he say?"

"Oh, he told Cindy something about how he wanted to talk to me. The same thing he said to me when I blew up at him in the English classroom." I turned and made an appeal to my brother.

"Bill, there's absolutely nothing for Jon and me to talk about! He is capable of doing great things in life, and he needs a girlfriend who's just as brilliant as he is. Like Claudia."

"Maybe he doesn't want Claudia. Did you ever consider that?"

I waved my soapy hands. "It doesn't matter. If he doesn't like Claudia, he can find someone else when he goes to Polytech. So can we please talk about something else?"

"I don't know," Bill said, deliberately baiting me. "You're such a worthless person that I doubt if we have anything to talk about, Kerry."

"Very funny." I went right on rinsing a frying pan.

"No, really. If I'm a superbrain like Jon, then I guess you don't want to be friends with me, either." Bill whistled a little tune as he poured himself a glass of juice. "And obviously I wouldn't want to associate with *you*. What have you ever accomplished in your life? I mean, except for being sweet and talented and caring, and fun to be with."

"Shut up, Bill."

"Seriously. Think about it. Are we going to start segregating people because of their intelligence quotients? Because if we are—"

"I told you to shut up, William Fields, and now you're going to get it!"

I was the one to grab the spray hose, and this time the water was going already. I squeezed the nozzle with great glee.

Bill got a good dousing. He didn't even try to take the nozzle away from me.

He just stood there, dripping all over the kitchen floor, and watched me as though I were a laboratory specimen.

"Well," he finally said. "I hope that helps get *something* out of your system, you little grouch. And now if you'll excuse me, I'm going to call Jon and tell him we'll have a telephone chess game from now on."

"Fine."

And they'll discuss me, I know they will, I thought bitterly. *But I don't care. Let them call me an airhead. I don't care a bit!*

Just as I had once gone out of my way to find Jon, I started to go far out of my way in order to avoid him. But it wasn't easy because now he was looking for me.

"Kerry?" His voice would come out of nowhere, while I was standing talking to my friends at school or when I was at my locker, choosing books for my next class. I'd turn and see Jon.

"Please, Kerry, just a short talk?" Jon would say, but I had already learned how to harden my heart against the wonderful sound of his voice.

"I'm awfully busy, Jon," I usually answered him, as politely as I could. "I really have no time at all for gabbing."

"But if you could just have a soda with me some afternoon, Kerry. It would only take five minutes."

"Gosh, I'm afraid I don't even have five minutes to spare," I'd say, sounding regretful. I never looked up into his face. I couldn't have stood my ground if I had seen the unhappiness in those wonderful gray eyes.

English class was the worst. I'd get my books ready before the bell and dash out the door as soon as the bell rang. I just kept hoping that he would give up and leave me alone at last.

A few times he telephoned me, but I made sure not to answer the phone. If my parents answered, they simply said, "Kerry says she doesn't want to talk with you, I'm afraid."

They hated doing that, but they respected my right to make my own choices, and they wouldn't lie for me.

If it was Bill who picked up the phone, of course he'd have a nice long chat with Jon. I could hear them blabbing away about their chess game and about Polytech and admissions and stuff. I'd leave the room while Bill was having those long talks with Jon.

Luke Russell was paying a lot of attention to me, and I was almost ready to give in and start dating him again.

"Come on, Kerry, we can double-date with Phil and Cindy again," Luke coaxed. "We can have a good time. How about if we went roller-skating and then for a pizza, maybe?"

But I ended up shaking my head. I'd already made up my mind at the Sadie Hawkins

Dance that Luke was not the boy for me. There was no sense in leading him on.

"I'll end up never marrying," I wrote in my diary one night as I sat cross-legged on my bed with Pillbox curled up beside me. "I'll lead a very glamorous life, jet-setting around the world—alone—with my camera and my magazine assignments."

But after I wrote that, I remembered how Jon had held my hand at the Polytech campus that night and how cherished I had felt when I believed that he cared for me.

"I suppose love is fine for some people," I continued to write. "And maybe—since it is an awfully nice thing to feel—maybe I'll continue to search for the perfect love for me."

Then I threw down the diary and the pen, and with tears in my eyes I gave Pillbox a violent hug.

"I miss him, Pillbox," I whispered. "I really miss him."

On Thanksgiving morning, I woke up early, knowing that Mom would need a lot of help with the holiday meal. We had tons of relatives coming over, and the turkey Mom was cooking was well over twenty-five pounds. Thanksgiving was her one big holiday to cook. Over the other holidays, we usually went out to visit my grandparents or aunts and uncles.

The morning went by fast, with all the last-minute cleaning and cooking. By noon, the crowds began to arrive. I have a lot of cousins, so our little house really began filling up with Fieldses and Murphys.

It was about two o'clock, and people were starting to take peeks into the oven to see whether or not the turkey was done, when one of my younger cousins came running into the kitchen.

"Kerry! Kerry, come quick!"

"What is it, Steffi? What's wrong?" I put down the sweet potato I had been slicing and followed her.

"Out there—on the front lawn!" Steffi said, pointing. I went to grab my jacket, but so many of my cousins were in the front hallway that I couldn't reach the coat closet.

"I think this delivery is for you, Kerry," said my cousin Maureen Murphy. She was five years older than I, and was someone I'd always looked up to. I wondered why she had such a mysterious smile on her face.

"I can't get near the door," I complained. Suddenly a path opened up for me. All my cousins, even the boy cousins who were usually big teases, were making way for me. And every one of them was chuckling—a lot.

"What's going on out there?" I pushed my way past the last of the cousins, and was finally able to see.

A brown VW Rabbit—Jon's mother's car—was driving back and forth in front of our house. Jon was tooting the horn and making an enormous fuss.

The car, practically afloat with multicolored helium balloons, had a large sign on it: PLEASE, KERRY, LISTEN TO ME FOR FIVE MINUTES.

"I don't believe this," I whispered. Jeremy and Joe, my twin cousins, who were about fourteen, were cheering wildly and clapping their hands at the ballooned spectacle. Then all my cousins started in. They were unmerciful.

"Whoever he is, listen to him, Kerry!"

"Aw, come on. Look at all the trouble he's gone to!"

"What kind of a monster are you, Kerry?"

I stood there feeling like an idiot, staring across the lawn at that silly car going back and forth. But the best was yet to come.

Jon stopped the car and stepped out, drawing cheers from all my cousins. "Hooray," they yelled. "Make her listen, man!"

Jon opened the back door and pulled out a huge basket that he had had on the seat. With a flourish he put the basket down on our front lawn—and out tumbled five fat, fuzzy puppies.

The puppies began scrambling every which way, but luckily enough people were milling around to make sure the pups were kept within the confines of our yard.

"Jon," I finally said when I found my voice. "What—what is this all about?"

He was grinning widely. Sure, he was firmly in control here. He had the support of so many of my relatives that it was unbelievable!

"Happy Thanksgiving, Kerry," he said.

Chapter Fifteen

Suddenly I started laughing. "You're crazy," I sputtered, while my cousins applauded and patted me on the back for being a "good sport."

"Did you think you had a patent on craziness?" Jon asked, reaching for one of the fuzzy puppies and plopping it into my arms.

"You seem to think you're the only one who can do nutsy things, Kerry. So I decided to show you that I'm not just a stuffy nerd after all. Behold. I can be certifiably insane, too." Before I could answer, he scooped up another puppy for his own.

"But—where did these puppies come from? And why?"

"They came from my neighbor; I borrowed them for a little while." Jon looked pleased and hopeful. "I knew that only drastic measures would get your attention, Kerry. And because it was you, I decided that puppies were the most logical way to be drastic."

"Puppies and balloons," said a cousin. "How romantic, Kerry. And he's pretty cute, too."

Steffi and the twins carried the other three puppies over and placed them at my feet.

"We like this guy, Kerry," said Steffi, and the twins echoed their agreement. "We think you should give him a chance!"

"Oh, definitely," said Maureen, followed by her sister Melinda. "This fellow has something to say to you, Kerry, and you've got to give him a break. It's only fair."

"I never knew I had such nosy cousins!" I howled, but I wasn't really upset. I was still laughing and struggling with the squirming puppy in my arms.

Jon was standing there patiently, watching me.

"Well—" I said. "Maybe just five minutes."

A chorus of cheers welled up on my front lawn. Bill, I noticed, was part of the crowd now, and so were my parents and aunts and uncles. If I was ever going to have any peace at all, I would have to give Jon those five minutes.

"You just get going," Maureen said encouragingly. "Don't worry. We'll all take care of helping your mother with the Thanksgiving dinner. Go on, go on."

"I have to get my jacket," I protested, but Maureen handed me hers, a beautiful, new corduroy jacket.

"No more excuses, Kerry," she said severely. "Your boyfriend has to take those puppies back, you know."

We took the puppies back in silence. I mean, we didn't talk much because we were trying to cope with a carful of tiny dogs.

"This reminds me of the first time we met," Jon said as he pulled into his street and parked at the neighbors' house.

"Yeah, I know. I know."

Jon said quietly, "I thought you were the most adorable girl I had ever met." Immediately he began collecting the puppies and plopping them back into the basket.

I just sat there, stunned.

Puppies returned, Jon drove toward the Polytech campus. The college was silent and empty because of the holiday weekend. I thought I knew where Jon was going, and I was right. He drove the car to the field where the human chess game had been played.

It was simply a long, vacant field now, with the grass turning brown from the frosty nights. With a little imagination, you could still see the chessboard and the royal players, strutting about in their exquisite costumes.

I have that kind of imagination. Maybe it's the artist in me, but I have a tendency to see ghosts in empty places, where an important event once took place.

I told Jon that. "Do you see them, too, Jon?" I asked. "Can you imagine them all right here, just as it was?"

"No," he said sadly. "Probably your friend Peter Ascari would, but I'm not that imaginative, I suppose. But that's just one of the things that makes us different, Kerry."

I sighed. *One of the many, many things that makes us different*, I thought with a sweet sadness.

"You wanted to talk to me for five minutes," I said, turning to face him. We were standing on the edge of the field, totally alone in the universe, it seemed. The wind was blowing at my hair.

"I brought you here to talk about chess," Jon began.

"Chess," I repeated, not quite believing my ears.

"Yes. Remember I said that chess is a fascinating game because at least two things are always happening at once?"

"Sure. You said that a person has to watch carefully or they might miss something important."

"And you kept asking me what I meant by that." Jon had his hands in his jacket pockets, and he looked uncomfortable, awkward. But he also looked determined to have his say, no matter what.

"I mean, Kerry, that there was you, running around all the time, climbing a tree, being cute and unconventional. And then becoming a lovely queen—"

"And a big flirt, in case you didn't notice."

"Oh, I noticed. But let me explain more. There was you being the way you are, on or off the chessboard, but then there was me, too. I'm always quiet, always a nerd. But always watching you, Kerry, and admiring you—"

"That's hard to believe."

"And always *loving* you, Kerry, even though I couldn't seem to show it." He gave a helpless shrug of his shoulders, and I noticed that his

163

face looked pale, when it should have been flushed out there in that windy, sunny field.

I was almost speechless. What he had said hit me with full force, just as though the wind had knocked me over.

"You were loving *me*? But I was so in love with you—and not because you were a handsome knight, but because you were you, Jon Madison. Only I kept fighting it because I'm too wacky—"

"That's nonsense, Kerry."

"So? Everything about me is nonsense. You said so yourself. I'm never serious, you said. And you kissed me goodbye because I was just a silly little person."

"I was wrong, Kerry." He held up his hands as if he didn't know how else to explain himself. "That's why I've been trying to talk to you all this time. But you wouldn't let me."

"I thought it would be better if we dropped the whole thing. I cared too much about you and you—you deserve someone like Claudia."

"Will you stop bringing up Claudia? There's nothing there, Kerry." He smiled thinly. "Look, you say you love me. Bill told me that you cared about me. Why are you being so stubborn? I know I'm a stuffy nerd, but I'm willing to try to change. . . ."

I stared at him.

"I don't want you to change. That's ridiculous. You've never been a stuffy nerd to me. I love you just as you are."

"Well. The same goes for me. I love your zaniness. From the first minute you drove me to school that day with the puppies, I knew that I was hopelessly in love. Can't you believe that?"

I absorbed what he'd said in silence. "So that's what you meant about two things happening at the same time on the chessboard. I was flirting with you and you were already—no, I can't believe it. You couldn't love me, Jon."

He put out a hand to touch my hair and pushed it gently back away from my face. "Come on, Kerry, believe me. I have to stretch my belief to realize that you weren't playing a game with me. Trust me."

"But—you're supposed to be the genius," I countered.

Jon smiled. It was the smile that I had seen in the photo. I'd been waiting a very long time to see that beautiful smile on his face.

"I'm not a genius in matters of the heart, I guess," Jon admitted. His hand was touching my cheek, as though I were someone very precious. "In fact, I've been awfully dumb about love."

He was really saying *love*. He was saying it to me! Something inside me began to soar with joy.

"And about those kisses," Jon went on. He pulled me close to him. "You said they were kisses I didn't mean. But you were all wrong."

Then, right there, overlooking the chess-board field, we kissed. This time there was no hesitation and no feeling that he was kissing me against his will. He didn't pull away, either, to tell me that I was a cute little person.

And there was something else. I didn't feel inferior this time, or tormented by doubts. I was thinking about what Bill had made me repeat: "I am Kerry, and I am a person of worth."

I didn't have to be afraid of Jon's intelligence. I was worth something because my life-style and my personality were my own. Take it or leave it. I didn't have to be afraid of being in his shadow. My photo had even been judged the best in the state, hadn't it?

I thought for a moment about all the cousins back at my house and how we would have to make a full report of all this to the Thanksgiving guests. Oh, well, Jon would be there to help me.

"Do you know what my two grandmothers are going to say about you?" I asked.

"Oh, no. What?" He looked worried.

"They'll say, 'Well, didn't we always say our cute little Kerry would be able to land a smart fellow?' "

Jon laughed. And I thought, *Sorry, Grandmas, I'm not trying to land anyone according to your plan. I'm just a girl in love, and Jon happens to be the boy I fell in love with!*

I had learned something about love. I knew now that one couldn't go around searching for a certain "type"—the artistic type or the nonintellectual type. When love happens, it just happens.

"Check," I whispered, when our second kiss was sweetly over. "Doesn't that mean that you're about to be captured?"

Jon hugged me tightly.

"I tip my king," he said in a quiet voice. "That means I surrender."

We hope you enjoyed reading this book. All the titles currently available in the Sweet Dreams series are listed on page two. They are all available at your local bookshop or newsagent, though should you find any difficulty in obtaining the books you would like, you can order direct from the publisher, at the address below. Also, if you would like to know more about the series, or would simply like to tell us what you think of the series, write to:

Kim Prior,
Sweet Dreams,
Transworld Publishers Limited,
61–63 Uxbridge Road,
Ealing, London W5 5SA.

To order books, please list the title(s) you would like, and send together with your name and address, and a cheque or postal order made payable to TRANSWORLD PUBLISHERS LIMITED. Please allow cost of book(s) plus 20p for the first book and 10p for each additional book for postage and packing. Please note that payment must be made in pounds sterling: Irish currency is not acceptable.

(The above applies to readers in the UK and Ireland only.)

If you live in Australia or New Zealand, and would like more information about the series, please write to:

Sally Porter,
Sweet Dreams,
Corgi & Bantam Books,
26 Harley Crescent,
Condell Park,
N.S.W. 2200,
AUSTRALIA.

Kiri Martin,
Sweet Dreams,
c/o Corgi & Bantam Books New Zealand,
Cnr. Moselle and Waipareira Avenues,
Henderson,
Auckland,
NEW ZEALAND.

SWEET VALLEY HIGH

Created by Francine Pascal
Written by Kate William

SWEET VALLEY HIGH is a great series of books about identical twins, Elizabeth and Jessica Wakefield, and all their friends at Sweet Valley High. The twins are popular, daring and smart—but Jessica is always scheming and plotting in ways only she knows how, leaving Elizabeth to sort out the mess!

Every story is an exciting insight into the lives of the Sweet Valley High 'gang'—and every one ends on a gripping cliffhanger!

So come and join the Wakefield twins and share in their many adventures!

Here's a list of all the Sweet Valley High titles currently available in the shops:

SWEET VALLEY HIGH SUPER SPECIALS

WINNERS

by Suzanne Rand

A great new mini-series . . .

Being seventeen can be great fun – as Stacy Harcourt, Gina Damone and Tess Belding discover as they enter their exciting senior year at Midvale High School. Apart from years of friendship, the popular trio share their main interests in common – an obsession with cheerleading in the elite school squad, and boys! For all three girls, the intricate gymnastic jumps and routines of their favourite hobby are the best things in their lives – but the gorgeous footballers they are supporting are definitely the icing on the cake! Picked to lead the cheering, the girls know they have one of the school's highest honours and a big responsibility to be the best that they can be in every way.

Each book highlights the story of one of the girls.

1. **THE GIRL MOST LIKELY**
2. **ALL AMERICAN GIRL**
3. **CAREER GIRL**

WINNERS – available wherever Bantam paperbacks are sold!